MISSION KASHMIR

MISSION KASHMIR

AN INTELLIGENCE MISSION IN THE VALLEY

LT. COL UDAYADITYA MUKHERJEE (RETD)

Srishti
PUBLISHERS & DISTRIBUTORS

Srishti Publishers & Distributors
A unit of AJR Publishing LLP
212A, Peacock Lane
Shahpur Jat, New Delhi – 110 049
editorial@srishtipublishers.com

First published by
Srishti Publishers & Distributors in 2023

10 9 8 7 6 5 4 3 2 1

Dedicated to the loving memory
of my father Arindrajit Mukherjee,
who inspired me to start penning my thoughts
from a very tender age.

And to few invincible men and women
in olive greens, for whom the
passion "India" is nothing but the elixir.

Acknowledgement

From mountains to deserts and jungles, to sleepy sea-side hamlets, living a life on the toes interspersed by periodic recoups in smaller towns is how most soldiers would like to define *fauji* life. Challenges and the grit to overcome them is what makes a soldier's experiences unique. When it gets tired of the malls and the departmental stores, the soul of a soldier craves to scale the lofty peaks or navigate through the maze of jungles and sand dunes. A soldier fights and endures both physically and mentally, sacrificing the bigger portion of his / her life for a greater cause. Children are born, they grow up, parents leave, grey strands appear unnoticed on the spouses' crop of hair and the soldier is just about there in the nick of time.

So, what do they do during all these times, except for guarding the nation? They build another family. A family with whom they spend the entire year, barring two months. The bonding in this family grows through participating in trainings and operations, doing academic courses, the formal and informal socializations and many such activities. No other profession can present such dynamic camaraderie and fellow feeling like the Army does.

Army made a soldier out of a casual "*Addabaaj*" Bengali youth in me and at the same time offered me ample opportunities to express my emotions on paper. This book wouldn't have been possible if twenty three-years back, I had given up during the training in Officers Training Academy (OTA) owing to the bone-breaking hardships. But it paid to survive and evolve. So here, raising a toast to all my fellow men and women in green and expressing my gratitude for the selfless service you are rendering to the nation that no amount of money can compensate.

The family of a soldier sacrifices a lot. For me, it was my parents and sister who would spend endless days and nights waiting to hear the one sentence – "You know what, I am coming home on leave". Having lost my father within a few years of donning the uniform, the bonding and longing to be with each other had grown even more sharply. Undoubtedly, it has been the love of my mother Uma Mukherjee and sister Ujjaini, to which I owe every single breath of my life. The designs of the almighty took shape in this world only because of their wishes for me. Had it not been for their sacrifices and support, I would not have even dreamed to write.

It is said that a person's future is shaped by the company he keeps in his or her formative years. I have been very fortunate to have grown with several exceptional minds in Ballygunge Place, the colony in Kolkata where I was born and grew up, and my school – South Point. Goes without saying, my childhood friends and my batch-mates in OTA influenced me a lot, which definitely gets reflected in my writing. A big thanks to you guys and gals.

Last, but not the least, I am extremely thankful to my publisher Arup Bose, who posed his confidence upon me as a writer of worth and guided tirelessly in bringing out this book. The painstaking efforts of Stuti and her team of editors helped me travel that extra mile to reach the platform where the readers now have the opportunity to savour and judge the inimitable story of Capt Zeenat, Zahir and Karim.

Foreword

"Hi Dada, what's up? I shall be passing through Kolkata next weekend. Let's catch up for a drink..."

The affectionate voice sounded from the other side on my mobile. Well, the enthusiasm and the warmth in the speech had not reduced a bit since the time we had sat shoulder to shoulder in a log hut somewhere in the north-east in the densely forested Myanmar border, awaiting fire from NSCN-IM militants several years back. I, then a green horn in the insurgency area, was impatient to fire at the faintly approaching murmurs, scattered and creeping up under the cover of the foliage. This man few years senior to me in service had lowered my barrel down and like Krishna would guide an uninitiated Arjun, had whispered in my ears,

"Hold bro...there is something called surprise and of course another thing called fire discipline...so wait till the attackers manifest their intent."

Well, what happened thereafter would be another story, but here this man who at one point of time was my mentor in the risk-prone service, Major Navjot (now Colonel Navjot) was going to be in town. Fifteen years had passed since we had shared a drink together. Owing to the vagaries of military service, physically we had not been able to catch up. A lot of water had flown along the various rivers across India and true to his mettle, Navjot sir was steadily climbing the ladder of hierarchy in the Army.

I had hung up my uniform for domestic compulsions and

settled down in my home town, Kolkata. So on this pleasant January evening we were seated across each other on the sprawling lawns of the Army Officers' Institute inside the Fort William garrison. We had lots to catch up with. We drank, raised a toast to old times, clinking glasses of our favourite Old Monk rum (that is what most troops and youngsters, years ago, used to find solace in after hours of gruelling treks chasing militants or climbing altitudes to keep the Chinese at bay from our frontiers).

After many a discussion, Navjot sir asked me a pertinent question. "Do you believe that writers have a responsibility towards society?"

"Yes. I have always believed that. The stories are a reflection of the conditions we live in. It has been so since time immemorial," I replied.

Navjot looked towards the greens of the golf course partly illuminated and rest absorbed in darkness. He seemed to be lost in thought for some time. Then he continued.

"I have read your books, Mukho. You have portrayed your experiences in the north-east. Rather picked up stories by your association with the people there. Why don't you write about something real from another part of the country?"

I asked him if he had any particular incident in mind, to which Navjot mentioned that he often felt that certain truth about the real story of Kashmir had not been told for a long time. He had served at least three tenures in various parts of the valley, including the current one, and was deeply in touch with the emotions and sentiments of the local people. He said that he had been witness to the changing times in the valley.

"As an author, your writings are not mere scripts; they are

chronicles of the times. Imagine a hundred years from now, how the generations would like to know about the times its forefathers had lived in?"

"There is this guy, Karim, you know, Mukho. He's a surrendered militant. His story is truly an eye-opener. It reflects what has been actually going on in the Kashmiri society for some time now. Would you like to listen to it?"

He stared at me intently. There was a depth in this man I had always admired. I had noticed that his actions and decisions in the thick of the strenuous situations, even as a young officer, were never typecast. He thought and acted with his heart. He was someone who would pause for moments, mentally deducing the consequences, before pressing the trigger of the rifle, even when death stared at him from a few yards away. You seldom get a thinker amongst the soldiers as the profession always thrives on a thin line between life and death, and afforded very less space to exercises one's thoughts. Navjot was a rare breed who had been gifted with the instinctive mastery of the art of discretionary thoughtfulness poised lightly on that thin line.

I smiled and quipped, "Sir, since when did you start giving me a choice?"

He laughed heartily and started narrating the true story of Karim and Zahir. It took us three sittings to collect all the nuances of the incidents. The more I progressed with the manuscript, I realised that it was different from the narration about the insurgency common people get to hear in the media. It was about the suffering of the people; people not only from the Indian side, but also from the other side of the LoC, who suffered and had endured the suffering for long. It was about the deceits and ploys of inimical agents who exploited people, governments and even the holiness in order to run an industry of hatred and earn wealth for themselves.

I had to change all the names of the characters in the story for the reason of safety and security of the people concerned. Also, I have fictionalised certain parts to keep the content more engaging for the readers.

1

The Rebirth

He was falling into a deep crevice. It was deep, dark and cold and there seemed to be no end. He did not remember exactly how long he kept falling into the abyss, but suddenly there was a booming voice echoing from somewhere. The voice was calm, serene and soothing. As he was alone in the darkness, the voice seemed to be an anchor, his only hope.

"Beta, souls are born as humans to live in goodness, peace and happiness...don't waste your life...Allah, the Almighty will protect you."

And then he found him being drawn back against the gravity of the precipitous tunnel and moving upward towards a night sky where a heavenly light shone and beckoned him to reach for the luminance, which seemed to be the source of the divine voice.

The voice faded, the light gradually disappeared and the eerie silence was soon replaced by beeps of electronic machines. Karim slowly opened his eyes as consciousness dawned upon him. His whole body felt numb, except for a tingling sensation at the bottom of his spine. He looked around. He was rested on a bed with a few monitors affixed on a table beside the bed. The beeping sound came from one such monitor. It probably read his pulse and BP, he realised through his daze.

A lady looked at him with a smiling face. Her face was hazy as Karim's vision was getting adjusted to the ambient light. "How are you doing?" the lady in the khakhi dress with epaulettes of a captain asked him.

"I am okay...but where am I now?" his voice was so feeble that he was barely audible.

"Relax...you are in the Military Hospital in Durgmulla. You were unconscious for the past seven days. I shall inform the doctor." The lady left the cabin leaving Karim scratching his memory. Gradually it started becoming clearer like the morning sunlight.

He started remembering everything.

But what is this happening? Why had they not killed me? The same people whom we were fighting brutally have turned out to be my saviours. So all that we had been thinking about this so called Jihad was turning out to be true. Karim tried to think of an explanation as his thoughts flew like a stream.

We..yes I, Zahir bhai and several others in our team who were compelled to fight a wrong cause – a lost cause. Where was Zahir bhai? I am alone in this cabin. Did he escape or was he killed? Will need to ask Abbu and Ammi. Will they be visiting me? I am not sure if the Army people informed my parents.

This much exercise by the brain had again started to make him feel dizzy. As he transcended the threshold of consciousness again into a state of distorted trance, a sharp voice shrieked in his ears...*"Tu bhaag, bhai...bhaag..."* And the scenes played on like a dream.

It was a cold, bleak day in the month of January. Dark smoky clouds hung over the crests of the Pir Panjal ranges which would start falling as flakes anytime they wished and cover the earth with layers of thick white snow. Zahir bhai had been ready since early morning. Ammi had told him to leave after having lunch, but he was getting impatient. Karim could sense it well. It had been a whole year since Zahir had been away from his parents and siblings. At twenty-two, a year younger than Zahir, Karim could correlate with his longing to be with his own folks. As Kashmiris, they were all very closely attached to their families and would hardly want to stay away from home for protracted periods. Also, the handler of crossings at the LoC had given a window of 10 a.m. to 10.30 a.m. for the exfiltration.

They set out around 9 a.m. from Karim's house in the village of Tekeri Wari. It would take about forty-five minutes to reach the ravine where Masood, the handler, would be waiting for them. He would guide Zahir along the path that followed upstream the *nullah* and then see him off at the narrow pass that opened onto a mountain grazing track leading down to the Neelum River. Zahir would cross the river on a makeshift bridge somewhere upstream and hit the road leading to Muzaffarabad. Once he crossed the river, he would be safe from Indian security forces. Zahir's village, Dossud was located in the Neelum Valley district and he would be home by lunch time, if all went off well.

As Karim's parents bid Zahir a teary farewell (and why not! He was amicable and lovable by nature) the two men slipped into their *phirans*, with the AK-47s slung across their chests. They commenced their journey. Karim would return home from the ravine after seeing Zahir off.

The steel of the barrel felt very cold under the phiran. It did not yield the warmth of senseless enthusiasm anymore and Karim hoped solemnly that it was the last day he was carrying it with him.

The area around the LoC was densely forested and patrolled by Indian Army columns frequently. These handlers who used to keep track of the patrols could predict the timeframe when a crossing would be possible. They were not accurate always and often *mujahideens* had been caught by surprise by the security forces. Many had lost their lives too. However, there was no other option to cross over for a Kashmiri from Pakistan occupied Kashmir (PoK). This chance had to be taken.

They reached the designated spot and Masood appeared from nowhere. He had probably been waiting nearby, camouflaged behind the dense foliage around.

"Salam Bhaijan, jaldi kijiye. Nobody knows when the Indian Army will come."

He extended his hand towards them. Zahir handed him a bundle of Indian currency. Ten thousand rupees. This was Masood's secret income, which aided him to construct a two-storey house in a village down below in the valley. Fortunately, he had not been caught by the security forces till then. He never got directly involved in acts of terrorism, but would rather act as a messenger and handler.

Zahir hugged Karim for the last time.

"*Khuda hafiz,* Karim. Take care of your parents."

His voice trembled. The man who sprayed bullets was not bereft of emotions. It was this soft element that differentiated

Zahir from radical maniacs and had enabled him to realise the truth about Kashmir quite quickly.

Suddenly something made Masood stiffen. From far off, there were sounds of dogs barking, coming closer. There was no village nearby. The dogs could only belong to the Indian Army's patrolling party.

Masood nudged at Zahir, commanding him to follow and asked Karim to leave immediately from the scene. They started climbing a goat track beside the stream. Karim decided to hide behind a huge oak tree as he wanted to be sure that Masood and Zahir crossed the ridge line safely. Karim had thought that the patrolling party would take some time before reaching the spot, even if they were headed towards them. But he was wrong. The barking grew louder and sooner than expected, a column of soldiers emerged on the track on which the three of them had been standing a few minutes ago.

They had heard the footsteps of Masood and Zahir who were about fifty metres from the ridge line. Owing to the sparse vegetation at that height, they were clearly visible to the column below. One of the soldiers shouted at them to halt. Karim waited with bated breath as he could see both the men pause and look down at the security forces. He was not certain if they would stop there or come down to be apprehended. If they kept climbing, it was beyond doubt that they would be chased and fired upon as anybody trying to reach the ridge line meant they were crossing over to PoK. And only fugitives or militants took this uncanny path.

One of the soldiers asked them to come down, pointing the INSAS rifle at them, while his companions took position on either side of the trail, scanning the area with strained eyes.

The buckled German shepherd was barking fiercely and trying to extricate itself from the hold of another soldier standing beside the one who had asked Zahir and Masood to stop. They were within the range of a hundred metres. Karim realised he had to do something and that too quickly.

It all happened in a flash. The man with the dog let it go and it started climbing up the path, barking fiercely. Karim unslung his rifle, took an aim in the general direction of the dog and fired. The animal, startled by the sound of the fire paused for few moments, but the soldiers caught the fume that trailed the fired bullet and hung in the air emerging from behind the oak tree. They fired back at the tree, and at the same time, Masood threw down two football sized boulders aimed at the dog and the soldiers. One hit the dog and it came down shrieking, panicked by the impact, while the two soldiers in front dived away from the path of the boulders.

Zahir yelled at Karim, *"Bhag ja! Bhag..."* and started climbing the remaining stretch along with Masood. Karim took advantage of the melee and ran into the narrow trail that ran zigzag beside the oak tree into the denser forests. The soldiers had gained their wits after being foxed for a few moments and fired indiscriminately behind him. They would soon catch up with Karim, who by now had lost his cool. Even while running, he started firing back, holding the rifle backwards from his shoulder, a technique he had learnt from Zahir. The bullets flew haywire over the heads of the chasing soldiers. Soon, a sharp object pierced Karim on the back of his left thigh and he stumbled over the root of a tree. It was a bullet. He had been hit. The descent was very steep and as he kept rolling down, the humming of the crickets and the rattle of the automatics faded. A darkness engulfed him and the only sensation he had before passing out was the cracking pain brought about by the sudden impact of his lower back hitting a hard surface as his body thudded to rest.

2

Story within the story

A week had passed since Karim had gained consciousness. The Army doctors and nurses really looked after him well. Karim often wondered why did they not just shoot him and add him to their tally of killed militants. He was, after all, a militant. Karim pondered that he had taken up arms to rebel against the country, a mistake which however had dawned upon him like broad daylight by then. And lying on a hospital bed looking at the sun-kissed greenery of the paradise on earth, he regretted the day he had taken the wrong decision.

The way these people in uniform have given me a second life proves that we were wrong in our thinking about them. Would I be able to forgive myself for all the bloodshed I had perpetrated against the same people who actually turned out to be my saviours? This only the Almighty Allah knew. He had a reason behind everything. Karim remained drowned in his musings most of the time.

His parents had started visiting him regularly. He had welled up seeing Ammi. Zubeida hugged her son and sobbed, "*Beta maine kaha tha aap ko galat raaste mat chalo.* Thank god for giving you another opportunity. Now try treading the path of righteousness."

After twelve days in the hospital, Karim was discharged. They thanked the military persons from the core of their hearts. When asked about the bills for the treatment, the military men said it was absolutely free. Karim's father had already planned to lease half of his farm lands to another wealthy family of the village in exchange of some money to meet the expenses. But the authorities refused. Karim had a broken ankle and a dislocated shoulder which had been operated upon and set. Fortunately, the bullet had failed to cause much harm as it had pierced his rear thigh muscle and remained lodged there without fracturing the femur. This treatment would have cost them in thousands in any private hospital. Just before leaving the hospital, a Colonel whom they had not seen before, came to speak to Karim.

His name tab read 'Manav Singh'. He congratulated Karim for his recovery and inquired about the family's well-being. After exchanging pleasantries, the officer politely informed that Karim would have to sign an undertaking of surrender and follow further legal formalities with the State police and judicial authorities. They had already seized the rifle Karim was carrying, which was Pakistan army issued equipment, marked accordingly. There was no denying the fact that Karim had taken up arms against India.

Karim was apprehensive about the interrogation by the Army and police as he had heard lots of gruesome details about the process. But the Colonel assured him that he would personally come over to Karim's place along with a small team and Karim would not be required to visit any place owing to his health condition.

Col Manav patted Karim on his back and said, "We, the Army people, are not going to trouble you, but you will have to face the police and court proceedings."

Karim looked relieved. He had already made up his mind to leave the path of militancy. Had this incident not happened, he would have thrown the rifle into the river and would have ceased to be associated with any person pursuing this useless cause.

Karim was happy to be back home. His movement was restricted and he would just lie down on his bed beside the window, witnessing the sky change colours over the lofty ridge lines. Along with them, the cliffs too would assume different moods. Sometimes they looked bright, happy and inviting, while at times as the sun kissed them goodbye, there would be shadows of melancholy draping down over them. This was further actuated by the tintinnabulation of the bells hanging around the necks of the sheep being driven back home. There was something with these lengthening shadows and the layered ringing sounds that filled the air with dejection from the surroundings as he would lie down with eyes closed. Zubeida would come with a glass of *kava* at this time and try to lift up his spirits.

The nights gave away to the bright mornings. The white clouds lazily ambled down the viridescent slopes of the mountains to spread like thin transparent layers of curtains on the valley, often trespassing through the window to softly caress Karim before dissipating away.

When they embraced Karim with their purity and freshness, ushering in a wild aroma soaked in permeating vapours, loneliness would step into the quaint quarters of solitude and the desolation would fade like the moisture melting as droplets of bliss, kissed by the soft rays of the gently smiling sun.

Karim often imagined a bright future for himself. He longed to lead a dignified life, marry and settle down with his family and make everyone happy. Then his thoughts would also cross the lofty crests across the valley in search of Zahir bhai, praying to the Almighty for a safe and secure life for him too.

3

Capt Zeenat

Somewhere in the state of Assam, where the majestic Brahmaputra swelled and heaved on its way towards further west, leaving clusters of lush green forests astride, a medium sized cantonment was witnessing a flurry of activities. Few men and a woman in their camouflage uniforms were looking at giant projection screens and discussing something agitatedly. Soon a man in his mid-fifties walked in and the group went silent.

"Yes guys, what do we have from the air?" Maj Gen D'souza demanded in his deep commanding voice.

The room housed the Image Interpretation Cell of the local formation, interpreting images captured by satellites and aired to troops on the ground. Very recently, there had been reports of Chinese patrol parties visiting one of the two disputed sites on the LAC, the fish tail areas. The eyes and ears of the Indian Army had picked this up and alerted the command centres located deep inside Indian territory.

For the uninitiated on the matters of military strategy and international relations, there are certain pockets of official disagreement between the Indian and the Chinese on the 4057 Km long LAC passing over the crests of the Himalayas, from Ladakh in the west to Arunachal Pradesh in the east. These places are covered by CBMs (confidence building measures), by accord of which troops from neither of the countries would occupy any posture there. Recently, Chinese troops have been seen thronging one of the pockets in an eastern valley of Arunachal.

Indian troops were positioned almost 70kms down south from the LAC and patrolled the area periodically to ensure no encroachment had taken place. The patrolling season is usually between April to September, as the rest of the time in a year, the super high altitude passes on the mountain ranges would remain covered under several feet of snow, rendering them inaccessible.

That year, the Chinese had kept visiting a pass on this fishtail area even in the month of November. The Colonel staff officer looking into the operations in the area rose up to brief the GOC (General Officer Commanding). He pointed at the projection screens and informed that successive patrols had visited the Cyang La pass between mid-October and mid-November. And what appeared from the pictures relayed by the satellite, the black dots on the slope below the pass on the Indian side looked like few small huts. The grazers never stayed so high up in the mountains, especially at that point of the year.

Gen D'souza keenly went through all the reports and dismissed the team. He asked the telephone operator to get him through to the Corps Commander stationed in an adjacent state, who was responsible for the defence of the eastern Arunachal.

"Jai Hind sir, the images aptly suggest some infra development."

"Are you sure they are not the grazing folks, D'souza?"

"Pretty sure sir, they are not."

"So what is your take?"

"Sir, we need to launch a patrol on foot."

"But it's all covered with at least 20 feet of snow there, D'souza. Add to that the chances of avalanches. Why don't we go for an aerial recce?"

"Sir, aerial recce by Air Force sorties so close to the LAC is risky. Even if they can be managed in the garb of training as per the CBM, the Chinese have to be informed beforehand. This would make them aware of our knowledge about their intention. We need to maintain surprise. Do not worry about the team, sir, we will select the best and train them quickly on winter survival skills."

"Ok. Start the preparations. Wait for my final confirmation. When do you plan to launch the team?"

"Sir, ten days from now."

The conversation ended.

A day later, a team of twenty soldiers were selected from an Infantry Battalion's commando platoon. These battle hardened troops remained ready to operate at short notice. The team would be led by an officer, Major Anish Reddy, who had adequate experience in high altitudes. The medic Capt Robin Dixit would also accompany the team. However, a problem occurred when it came to depute another officer as the deputy team leader, second in command to Maj Reddy. The GOC wanted an officer from the image interpretation team to accompany the patrol and be the second in command (2IC) of the patrol. But Maj Gaurav Singh, the intelligence officer had some sudden domestic compulsion and had to proceed on leave.

Capt Zeenat, the officer who had assisted Gaurav in the image interpretation volunteered to be a part of the mission. The commanders at higher levels were quite skeptical about sending a lady officer with barely two years of service on a mission to one of the most treacherous terrains in the world. The issue was not about the professional capability of the officer, but her comfort zone in an all-male operational team. While the seniors toiled with the idea, Capt Zeenat sought for an interview with the General through proper channel.

The GOC met the young officer in his office. Zeenat mentioned to him that hailing from Kashmir, she had been born and brought up in the midst of mountains, passes and wild streams.

"I can climb the heights better than most men sir, and that also with the battle gear."

Gen D'souza stared at the officer for few brief seconds, appreciating the gumption the young soldier was showing. She reminded him of his twenty-year-old daughter completing her education in the confines of a cozy home in Bangalore. This girl would be only a few years elder than his daughter Rose.

"I don't doubt your physical capabilities or professional competence, Zeenat. In fact, having someone from the IIT serves our purpose. But will you be comfortable to fend for yourself in the wilderness? Living off the land, sleeping in open, hygiene issues – these may be challenges you have to encounter more than climbing slopes and crossing streams." D'souza was as candid as possible.

"Sir, if a woman is not safe with her brothers in arms around, where else can she feel safe? I have served with them for the last couple of years, played with them, ran with them, dined with them and spoken the rustic rural dialects. The bonhomie and camaraderie I share with our men are much deeper than those I have shared with any lady. I am as much a soldier as they are. Please do not deny me this mission." Zeenat spoke at a breath's length.

D'souza commended the girl's spirit.

"You know Zeenat, the Army does not treat men and women differently in matters of soldiering. You all are equally trained to stand up to any challenge. We were just worried about the comfort level. However, I have made up my mind. Join the pre-induction training from tomorrow." He smiled to dismiss the young officer.

Zeenat smartly saluted the General and walked out of his office.

After a training of ten days on high altitude trekking, negotiating of obstacles, communication methods and other aspects, the patrol had been airlifted to an Assam Rifles (a paramilitary force operating in North East under the operational command of Indian Army) post situated on the middle altitudes of the eastern Himalayas in Arunachal.

The post commander, Major Barun Chatterjee left no stone unturned in looking after the members of the patrol team which would stay there for two days, carrying out final preparations before setting off on the arduous trek. The post was located in a small bowl like feature, at an altitude of

4500 feet, surrounded by lofty peaks all around. The peaks were all snowcapped and changed colours with change in direction of the sun shining brightly atop in the pristine blue winter skies.

Zeenat, the deputy leader of the patrol, had stared at them and wondered what lay beyond. They would have to skirt these peaks through valleys and meadows, climb a few of them where no passes existed and reach the LAC almost 70 Kms away. The distance and the height differential of almost 12000 feet between the post and the pass on the LAC would be covered over a period of ten days one way. The team would reach the base of the pass and establish a patrol base. The earlier patrols had reported that the gradient from the base to the pass was extremely steep and required tremendous endurance and skill to ascent. From the patrol base, the team would recce the pass and the adjoining area over two days, divided into two subgroups on two consecutive days, and then start returning, unless there would be confrontation with the PLA troops.

One of the most important parts of planning the mission was hiring porters. The local youths had always been supportive of the Indian Army and willingly offered their services as load bearers. They would carry the rations, portable bivouacs, medicinal kits, etc., and would be very handsomely paid for their services. Another benefit from these people emerged in the form of navigational skills. Though the patrol would progress from point to point with the help of maps, compass and the GPS, the latest information about the topography were available with these local people. They grazed sheep and ventured deep inside the forests for hunting and always could guide the faujis on streams having changed course, decimation of a track owing to landslides, level of snow at different places and many other aspects.

A total of twenty porters had been kept ready by Major Chatterjee. Anish and Zeenat interacted with them and gathered information on the latest condition of the tracks. The loads were distributed evenly, where each would require to carry ten to fifteen kgs. Zeenat was surprised to find a pair of girls in the team of the porters. When she inquired if girls would be allowed to work as porters, Barun Chatterjee smiled and said it would not be an aberration to say that the women in these regions were physically and mentally sturdier than men.

Aliang and Reliang, the two girls in their early twenties, dressed in oversized pullovers and track pants smiled shyly at Zeenat.

"Tum log jaa sakega fauj ke sath? (Can you people walk with the Army?)," Zeenat had asked them.

They had jointly replied that if Zeenat could take the arduous trek, what was different with them. They further added that it was the first time they had seen a lady officer going for a patrol in this area. But in their opinion, looking at Zeenat's physical standard, they were confident that she could do this patrol successfully.

Zeenat had smiled and could not help but like the duo for their enthusiasm and cheerfulness.

The patrol started on the designated day. The team had moved from bound to bound. These were known as patrol stages and were generally flattish areas beside some river or stream. Few had very old rickety bamboo frameworks over which the patrol team could hang the tarpaulins or plastic sheets for shelter. Few had thatched huts too, which required maintenance. Zeenat gathered that the last patrol to this sector had been about a year-and-a-half back. The harshness of the terrain coupled with the inclement weather made several kilometres on either side of the LAC inhospitable and inaccessible. There were no human presence and it was an accepted fact that neither country would develop any infrastructure in the zone. Once in a while, the patrols of both the countries would carry out an area domination and return to respective bases. The Chinese had probably taken advantage of that posture and intruded inside Indian territory, which was required to be found out.

The patrol had followed the hunting track and traversed mountainous terrain through ascents and descents, though Zeenat could understand they had been actually gaining altitude. Anish had suggested her to carry a pistol as a personal arm if she wanted, but Zeenat had insisted on carrying an AK 47 rifle like the other members of the team. She had realized soon that it was not at all an easy task to climb the steep gradients of fifty to sixty degrees at places with the rifle weighing about five kilos and the personal kit rucksack. It called for stretching the physical capacity, but she took solace in the fact that even the men found it challenging. And also she would keep drawing inspiration from Aliang and Reliang, who walked effortlessly with loads tied on their backs, yet had a smile on the lips always. Both the girls had taken a liking for Zeenat and stuck to her while walking and resting.

One incident especially had etched an indelible impression on Zeenat's mind. There was a stream en route which had considerable volume of fast flowing water. It was wide and could not be waded through. It had to be crossed by something the locals called “Tawa”. It was a harness hung around a metallic rope tied to trees on either side of the stream. The slings attached to the harness were connected with a concave wooden contraption that rested on the rope. A person had to use the harness as a sit, hold the wooden contraption and slide down the rope to the other side. The main challenge would be going forward from midpoint of the rope as it was against the gravitational pull, courtesy the curvature of the rope.

It had taken immense effort for Zeenat to cross over, especially to slide across the second half of the rope which was an upswing towards the far bank. With the rifle tied across her chest and the rucksack mounted on her back, Zeenat had ardently monkey crawled the distance, putting all the strength of her arms and legs behind the effort. Aliang, Reliang and the troops cheered her as she finally reached the other end and had slopped on the ground in a heap of flesh, bones and clothes with no sensation remaining in her body. She had trembled for minutes through her numbness before gradually recuperating and gaining back her strength. Major Anish patted her on the back as she had stood up gaining her composure and complimented her on the sheer stamina displayed by her.

The radio operator, Vignesh had got stuck in between and could proceed no further with the heavy radio set on his back. Zeenat observed with awe how Reliang swiftly crawled with her arms and legs to the spot on the rope, unhooked the radio set to fasten it across her back and pulled Vignesh by entangling his waist with her strong pair of legs.

Zeenat had felt the pride of being a woman swell up through her chest by this scene. The scenario had prompted a strange motherly instinct in her, where the postures of the two in the act of rescue portrayed an abstract imagery of a mother carrying a baby in her womb before delivering through months of laborious effort.

She had hugged Reliang affectionately, who panted heavily after the act, as the male gazes flew at them with respect, reverence and admiration. The proud womenfolk had chirped gaily as they had resumed the journey.

Lying in her dingy polythene bivouac at night, Zeenat used to get absorbed in the surrounding ambience. Hills, green meadows, gorges, rivers and the flora and fauna were nothing new to her having been born and grown up in Kashmir. But these parts of the Himalayas seemed to be more primitive. They were shrouded in mysteries since time immemorial, impregnable fortresses of untouched and virgin foliage where the morning dew trickling down the mossy brown barks of the tall deodars and oaks seemed to have been sipping in since the time of birth of these forests. Compared to Kashmir, this region was sparsely populated and large parts of these lands had remained unexplored by humans. The air was fresher to inhale and laden with unknown aromas that had a calm, meditative effect on the entire being of a person. As Zeenat would doze off with her head rested on the rucksack, feeling assured by the rifle by her side, the burble of the small rivulets and ubiquitous nocturnal sounds of nature that felt like crooning by heavenly angels at times, would transport her to realms of the dreamland. Aliang and Reliang who used to share a small tent pitched beside Zeenat's, would describe these sounds as merriment of beings from other world who inhabited the higher reaches of the mountains astride the camping sites. Zeenat would laugh yet never rebuff the simple beliefs of these innocuous souls.

As per the patrol schedule, the team had reached the base of the pass after ten days of strenuous journey over the treacherous terrain. The base was located at an altitude of 14500 feet on a ledge of the ridge line that tapered to a vertical wall of almost 70 degrees gradient. The upper portion of the wall, another thousand feet above, remained veiled by wet mist and the porters said that it opened into a gradual uphill slope leading to the pass on the ridge line known as Cyang la Pass. The territory on the other side of the ridge belonged to Tibet Autonomous Region (TAR), a precinct acceded by China.

There were patches of snow everywhere, but they seemed to have fallen several days earlier. It had not snowed recently, which was a big relief for the team. The vertical rock face did not have any snow covering as it was not possible for it to accumulate on such a steep slope. But the surface was slippery with water melting from the snow mass above, trickling down over the crusts of mosses and algae. The wall had little foothold.

Two porters prepared cane ropes from bamboo stems collected from a nearby grove. One of them climbed up the rock face stepping on small rocky protrusions and tied one end of the rope on a clump of bushes jutting out from the surface. The second porter then climbed up holding the rope and created footholds on the wall at regular intervals by striking the rock with his pickaxe.

The first batch comprising of Maj Anish and ten soldiers had climbed on the first day of the scheduled recce of the pass. Zeenat would visit the pass on the next day, accompanied by the medic and the balance troops. She saw the team onerously negotiate the rock face and vanish into the misty cliff. It took tremendous effort to climb with the rifle slung across the back. One after another, they traversed the altitude smoothly, courtesy their mountain craft training, except for one soldier. Pawan Singh, a rifleman, slithered down the rope after his feet slipped on the wet surface at a height of thirty feet. Fortunately, the rope helped him to arrest the fall and prevented any serious injury. Zeenat realized it would require not only physical strength, but a whole lot of focus and concentration. Whatever it would take, she was ready for the challenge and resolved to complete the task without fail.

The team came back after about four hours. They had clicked photographs. The pass was under several feet of snow. The structures that the satellite imagery had picked up were heaps of stones erected by the Chinese. They had painted them yellow and written "PLA", "this is Chinese territory" and "India go back" on them. From the satellite, these had looked like houses. There were many Chinese telltale signs like empty cigarette packets, toffee wrappers and juice cans found littered across the place. The Chinese had visited recently.

Next day early morning Zeenat, Capt Robin and the remaining ten soldiers climbed to the pass. Zeenat did not find it as difficult as it had seemed from below. Her supple frame could lift itself quickly, stepping from stone to stone, gaining just adequate toeholds. She had remembered three golden principles of cliff climbing taught to her by her grandfather as a child. “Never pause in between, concentrate the body weight on the toes and never look down.”

Zeenat had found that the stone structures had been dismantled by Maj Anish’s team the previous day. The Chinese items had been collected, and instead, there lay empty packets of Indian noodles, cigarettes and chocolates. The feature, approximately one hundred square feet, was concave in shape, with boulders strewn around. At the far end, a track seemed to have gone down towards the Chinese terrain, which was comparatively lesser in gradient.

Zeenat and team further patrolled the area for some time when suddenly the sentry who had been keeping a watch on the Chinese side mentioned that he had spotted few people approaching the pass. Zeenat, being the leader of the team, had to take a call whether they should retreat or stay put. She had quickly looked at the group through the binoculars. As the shapes kept growing bigger, it was certain that those were soldiers of the People’s Liberation Army (PLA).

Zeenat alerted Maj Anish, who was at the patrol base, and in no time, the Chinese patrol consisting of twenty troops had reached the pass. They deployed themselves tactically, rapidly encircling Zeenat’s team. Two men wearing shoulder titles of a Major and a Captain approached Zeenat and Capt Robin, who were standing in the middle of the snowy patch. The Chinese wore stern expression on their face which gradually gave way to surprise and then cynicism after seeing a lady officer. It would take Anish’s team at least an hour to reach up to the pass. Till then, Zeenat,as the deputy leader of the Indian patrol would have to engage with them.

The Chinese Major spoke in a broken and accented English.

"This is China zone. You go back."

Zeenat observed that though the patrol was armed with Chinese AK 56 rifles, they were not very aggressive in their attitude. Instead, they probably wanted to convince the Indians to evict by talking. Zeenat had prepared herself mentally for all eventuality, but decided not to resort to fire arms unless provoked by the Chinese. Her voice echoed between the ridge lines as she shouted her orders to the troops scattered around on the pass.

"Koi fire nahi karega jab tak yeh log kuch karte nahin."

Then, she firmly spoke to the Chinese officers.

"You are in Indian territory guys. Please go back. The Chinese territory starts beyond the track."

The Chinese Major mumbled something which Zeenat could decipher as "No man's land".

She asked them to go back, as neither country could have any construction or presence on No Man's Land. But the Chinese troops remained wherever they had taken positions. The Captain took out a packet of cigarettes and after lighting a couple for them, extended the packet towards Zeenat and Robin. As both of them declined, the Chinese took few steps back and kept talking with each other, puffing away thick smokes, adding to the layers of mist that kept rising from the lower heights.

The stalemate continued for a while, with both the patrols holding on to their positions. Then as the Chinese Captain, who was more casual than his senior in his demeanour, approached Zeenat asking if they were carrying Indian Rum, the figure of Maj Anish and another soldier emerged from the mist behind. Gradually, the balance of the patrol had also reached the pass and taken position all around, marking each Chinese soldier.

The Chinese Major who had smoked a few cigarettes by then, marched ahead to meet Anish. He intimated that they did not want a fight, but demanded the Indians to retreat immediately. Anish replied to him by saying that the Chinese had constructed stone pillars on the pass, hence they had come to check. He further added that the Indians would leave the moment Chinese left the pass and went back to their side of the LAC.

Almost two hours had passed and it was freezing at the pass. Zeenat could feel the fingers and the toes turning numb inside the gloves and the shoes. It was decided that one by one, the troops from both sides would start moving out of the pass. The simultaneous action started while the officers waited to leave at the last. All of a sudden, the Chinese Captain approached the three Indian officers and shook hands with them. When he reached Zeenat, he flayed his arms and tried to hold her in a bear hug. Zeenat had not expected this antic, but her womanly instinct further accentuated by the trained reflexes prompted her in taking two quick steps back and proffer the barrel of the rifle towards the man. The swiftness of her response and the steel poking at his belly had flummoxed the Chinese Officer. Two Indian soldiers awaiting nearby for their turn to evacuate had immediately caught hold of the Captain by his shoulder and dragged him away. All this happened quite fast. Seeing this, a couple of Chinese soldiers dashed at the Indian men, screaming what seemed to be profanities in Chinese. Before the troops broke into a fist fight, the Chinese Major commanded the troops in a raised voice. They stopped and disengaged from the Indian men's strong embrace. Anish too instructed the men to step back.

The Chinese men cast a last glance to the Indians and turned towards their territory. Anish, Zeenat and the soldiers, who had caught hold of the Captain, followed them till the end of the pass and waited before the patrol melted away into the thick fog creeping up the Chinese slopes. It was certain that the Chinese had built some infrastructures somewhere nearby in their territory, which had not been picked up by satellites yet. They could see the Indian patrol on the pass from a distance and rushed to the pass to confront. Anish mentioned that the higher headquarters would decide based on the reports submitted by them.

The patrol rested for a day at the base before starting back on their journey. After a similar trek of ten days, the patrol was greeted by Maj Banerjee and the troops of Assam Rifles. The mood was jubilant and Zeenat could see the respect and reverence for her in the eyes of the troops and hear the same in the sublime whispers hanging in the air around her. Before departing on a helicopter, Zeenat had hugged Aliang and Reliang. They promised to keep in touch with her and meet if they would come down to Assam any time soon.

The difficult patrol was a success. Zeenat earned rave laurels for her grueling grit and guts in completing the patrol and lead the men on the pass as a deputy leader. She was commended with a gallantry award, Sena Medal, making her one of the youngest woman officers in the history of Indian Army to receive one. And the icing on the cake was delivered in the form of a posting to her home state Kashmir, with the reporting date for the new assignment fixed after a couple of months.

4

New assignment - Kashmir

It had been a few months since Zeenat had been posted to Kashmir, her home state. This meant she would be able to spend some more time with her family, at least for the next couple of years. The Army would also be able to utilize her knowledge about the local populace and the culture.

One evening, she had returned from an exhilarating game of basketball. It was the final match of the Inter-Unit basketball tournament of the formation and her team of the Division troops had won the final match after defeating an Infantry unit team. It was a first in the history of the formation. Being one of the two female players, the other one being Capt Alka Dimri, playing vigorously dashing shoulders with male players, they had won a huge round of applause from the spectators. The GOC praised Zeenat in front of everybody and made a special mention of the two lady players during the presentation ceremony.

It was indeed a very happy moment for her, especially so when she was primarily instrumental in the victory of her team, filling the basket at least a dozen times. However, from a gender point of view, she remained unfazed as she never considered herself any different from men physically or mentally since her childhood. In college too, she played basketball and volleyball with her male counterparts and had participated in many state level tournaments representing her college. Had her home state not been under this kind of turmoil for so long, she would definitely have represented the Indian national team. She could try now, but with a full-fledged career in the Army, deployed in counter insurgency operations, it would be a difficult proposition. She loved her job and did not want to compromise it by taking up basketball more seriously, which otherwise the organization would have been quite happy to support. At twenty-eight, age was also not on her side, she felt.

Zeenat requested for a glass of fresh lime juice from the officers' mess over the intercom and took a hot shower. She was looking forward to her 'me-time' as she wanted to read an interesting book that she had borrowed from the library.

She stretched her legs on the couch in the drawing room of her two-room kitchenette apartment accommodation meant for single officers and flipped through the pages of the book, *The Alchemist* by Paulo Coelho. She had this habit of flipping through the pages of a book before starting to read it. She picked up the glass of juice and her gaze for the umpteenth time fell on the photo frame kept on the side table. She had got the photo framed during her last leave in Srinagar. The Mirza family; her family. The happy faces of her Abbu, Ammi, sisters Nusrat and Rubayat, her toddler nephew Mir and brother-in-law Ehsaan. This picture had been shot seven years back. A lot had changed since then, and one of them in the photograph watched them from the heavens. Her *bema* or brother-in-law Ehsaan was no longer with them. The pain still sprang up from the deepest corner of her heart in moments like these. She tried to grapple with the options she had had to save him on that fateful day. She found herself getting lost in her own stream of thoughts. From one to another, her thoughts splashed like the waves of the sea she had seen in Chennai's Marina beach, before receding away to get lost in the vast repertoire of the reminiscences.

Suddenly, the phone rang and brought her back to the present. The exchange operator spoke on the other side,

"Jai Hind Madam, Col Manav Sahab baat karna chahte hain."

Soon after a hold of few seconds, the affectionate and deep voice of Col Manav sounded on the other side.

"Hello Zeenat, great match. You vanquished the opponents single handedly. They did not know what had hit them."

Zeenat felt her spirits rise being praised by the senior.

"Thank you, sir. Good to see that I have not lost my moves," she replied.

"Okay listen, remember we discussed about this Kashmiri guy called Karim who was apprehended by the Army during a crossing over incident? He was in hospital and has been discharged a few days back. I want you to come along tomorrow for a chit-chat with the boy. I shall send across the vehicle around nine in the morning to pick you up," Col Manav explained the purpose of his calling.

Zeenat being a Kashmiri was always a big help in interrogation sessions. And she enjoyed this job.

"Roger sir. I shall be ready. Jai Hind!" Zeenat placed the receiver back after Col Manav had signed off with a 'Jai Hind'. New assignments were always challenging. And challenges made her happy.

5

Karim's house

After a fortnight, one fine morning, Col Manav accompanied by a young lady visited Karim. His parents received them warmly and following a round of *chhir chot* and *kahwa,* they wanted to speak to him in isolation. Karim was still restricted to his room and his parents left, closing the doors behind them.

"*Karim aap shuru se batayei kaise aap militants ke saath mile.* Tell us everything. Whom you were in touch with and where they are now. Do not worry as you must have known by now that our aim is not to kill you people, but enable everyone like you to return to a normal life."

Col Manav had an air of assurance that made Karim willing to trust his words. He came across as a kind of person whom one would like to trust one's life with.

The pretty lady reaffirmed Col Manav's words and introduced herself as Captain Zeenat from the Indian Army. She narrated how her brother-in-law had been caught in a cross fire between the army and the militants and had died. After that, the Army helped her poor family, ensuring Zeenat who was the second eldest among three sisters and a graduate, join the Army as an officer. She had trained for a year at the Officers Training Academy in Chennai, spent a couple of years in Northeast India before getting posted to the valley.

Karim stared at the lady in bewilderment. The physically fit young woman looked smart in the Army's camouflage uniform. He had heard of big Indian cities and felt a tinge of jealousy for Zeenat. She would be few years elder to him, but led such a dignified life, full of travelling, different experiences while he was wasting his, lying injured on a bed in the confines of the small house in his village.

Karim took out a leather-bound diary from under his pillow. The words 'Zahir Nama' were inscribed in a calligraphic handwriting on the white cover. It was the chronicle of the young man, Zahir from across the border who had initiated him on the path of so-called jihad. Zahir had forgotten to pick it up while leaving for his village across the LoC and left it behind. Karim had kept it secured with a hope that someday he would be able to dispatch it back to Zahir. It contained the events that led Zahir to join the ranks of the militants and the journey of his thoughts from radicalism to the essential truth – the enlightenment in his own words that made him decide to go back to his people and choose a path of peace.

"If you want to know my story, then it is best to start with this diary. It speaks of the story of going astray as well as the journey back to the path of righteousness. I will narrate the rest of it," Karim handed over the diary to the officers.

As it was written in Urdu, Zeenat took it from him and started reading it aloud.

6

Zahir's Diary

How I became the chosen one

25th March

It was ten in the morning. I had come back from the grazing grounds in the valley that sprawled by the small river below our village Dossud. As I climbed the pebbled stairways that led to our house lodged on a green ledge in the village, I could hear voices coming from the verandah in front of the house. When I landed on the small flat piece of land in front of the house, I saw two persons sitting in front of my father Liaqat and elder brother Ibrahim. My mother Salma stood behind the door with a tray of kahwa. I took it from her and served the guests. One of the men was a *maulavi* and another seemed to be a Pathan sporting a sherwani. The maulavi beckoned me to his side and patted me on my back.

"Kitna honhar naujawan hain...Allah Tala ko aise hi bande chahiye. Allah needs young and intelligent men like him for Jihad."

Then he continued addressing my father. *"Aap paanj dafa*

namaz toh adah karte honge. Allah Tala pe bharosa toh hoga? Toh phir ek dindan mussalman hone se aapka farz banta hain ki aapke ek bete ko Allah ke rah par saunp de. (You must be offering prayers to the Almighty five times a day. You must have full faith in god. Then being a devout Muslim, it is your duty to offer one of your sons to the path of god.)"

I could not understand. The Pathan then took over from the maulavi and explained that they were recruiting young men from various villages for joining a training camp run by the outfit Lashkar-e-Taiba and assisted by the Pakistan army somewhere near Muzaffarabad with the aim of liberating the Indian state of Kashmir from the clutches of the oppressive regime. I had heard a little bit about the issue. Frankly, I was not interested in these things, and hardly read the newspaper. Few years back, students in our secondary school used to talk about problems the Kashmiris were facing on the other side of the border. However, we were living peacefully and contented on this side of the border.

The Pathan guy whose name I came to know as Bilawal, took out a small video camera and started playing clips urging all of us to watch. "*Dekhiye, kis tarah aziyat dala jaata hain Kashmirion par...* (Just see how Kashmiris are tortured.)"

I must say we had never seen such traumatic and brutal clips of torture. Uniformed men spanking nude youths by hanging them upside down from the trees. Old men being hit by butts of rifles and many other tormenting sights went on one after another. Though in all the clips, the visuals were a little hazy, they were blood boiling beyond doubts. In one particular video, I found fair skinned kids being booted and spanked by soldiers who were very dark complexioned. When

I pointed this out, the maulavi said that the people from India generally had complexions like that. I did not question him further.

He had went on to add that it was our duty to avenge this torture against our own people by infidels. The Almighty would not pardon us if youths keep sitting idle, even after seeing all this.

We all were deeply disturbed and infuriated by the scenes. My father stood up and held the hands of the maulavi. My father was a soft person by heart. He was god fearing and religious by nature. Not formally educated other than in the Quranic scriptures, he was a typical village shepherd who toiled hard to look after his family consisting of six children and wife very well.

Tears were rolling down his cheeks. He expressed his anguish and said that if it was for a noble cause, he was ready to send one of his sons to fight the tyrants. He looked at me and directed me to be a soldier of the jihad to end oppression and save my own people from peril.

I myself was convinced that I would dedicate myself for the holy war against the enemies of our people and Islam. I asked Bilawal what I needed to do. He replied that within a week, somebody would come and guide me to the training camp, where I would be taught weapon handling, firing, jungle tactics, communication and other techniques for operating inside India and fighting the Indian security forces.

7

Zahir's Diary

At the training camp
2nd May

Today after almost after a month, I have got time to write in my diary, again. The last one month passed by in the blink of an eye it seems.

I had started out from home on 31st March. Two people had come to escort me to the training camp. My parents had hugged me and wept like children. It had melted my heart, but I had steeled myself remembering the gruesome videos we were shown a few days back. My mother tied a *tabij* (sacred pendant) around my upper arm on the right hand and said,

"Beta Allah ne aapko mujhe diya tha aur main Allah ke hukm par aapko Un ke rah me bhejh rahi hoon. Jahan bhi raho salamat raho aur humesha sacchai ke sath dena...Jihad buraiyon ke khilaaf hota hain... majhabi gunaah ke khilaf hota hai...aur majhab sacchai ke buniyad par kayem rehta hain...

(Son, the Almighty had given you to me and I am giving you back to His cause. Now I'm sending you on His path. Stay safe wherever you go...always be truthful. Jihad is against immorality. It is against deviation to religion and religion is based on the pillar of truth.)"

As we hit the highway from our village, I saw there were three more youths like me, escorted by two other jihadis headed for the same destination. We travelled on the express bus service and reached the town of Balakot in Pakistan, situated very close to the border between Azad Kashmir and the North West Frontier Province of Pakistan. We travelled on foot from the bus stand and after walking for ten minutes through hilly tracks, reached a jihadi madrasa situated on a flat area jutting out from a ridge line. This was away from the main town and surrounded by dense foliage.

The madrasa was a three-storeyed building. It had a huge courtyard in the centre, surrounded by rooms on three sides. All the rooms opened to continued balconies on all floors facing the courtyard in the centre. There were plenty of rooms of different sizes, including kitchens and living quarters. We were provided big rooms on the second floor designed as dormitories. Seven to eight persons were allotted to each of these rooms. There were camp cots with thin mattresses, pillows and a thick blanket on each. I had never seen such soft colourful blankets earlier; we used sheepskin rugs and blankets in our houses which were coarser than these. One of the boys commented that they were from China.

These dormitories did not have any other furniture and the closed windows which had been sealed by iron wires made the air suffocating. We were strictly told not to open the windows. I resolved myself thinking about the noble cause that I had joined to serve and believed that any hardship on this path was just. After a hot meal that comprised of roti, *gosht* or lamb meat and *firni,* a dessert prepared with rice, milk and dry fruits, we retired for the day. Every day, we had plenty to eat and I would often feel sad remembering the frugality of the meals my family shared back home.

Our training started from the next day. We were a batch of twenty-five young men assembled from various parts of Kashmir and Pakistan. At the very beginning, we were addressed by a man called Abu Musafir. He declared himself as the camp commander and delivered a fiery speech on how the Indian Kashmiris were being brutalized by the *Kafir* Indian Government.

"Woh Kashmirion ka nasal badalna chahte hain par Khuda gawah hum une hi barbad kar denge. In zahil kafiron ka naam o nishan mita denge...Islam pe jo waar karega unko khatam kar dena hi nek aur paak zimmedari hain. (They want to change the race of the Kashmiris, but in name of Allah we will destroy them. We will annihilate these bigot infidels. It will be the most divine and righteous duty to kill all those who are the enemies of Islam.)"

I felt goosebumps on my skin. Abu kept pacing in between the ranks of the men seated in the big courtyard inside the madrasa. He spoke and made it a point to pause in front of each one of us and look into our eyes as if passionately trying to drill in the words. The fire that spewed out of his kohled eyes glaring over a hawkish nose, the high pitch of the voice, the thick pungent fragrance of the *itr* (perfume) and the fanatic mannerism of this man somehow had started running in our veins. We were hypnotised, swaying with a blind rage fomenting inside us. Our senses had been pervaded by this hysteria and the tempo built up with the hall resonating with the repeated cries of *'Allah hu Akbar...Jihad Zindabad.'*

We were shown more videos of torture on Kashmiris in India and our young blood boiled with anger and resentment. How could a country inflict such inhuman atrocities on its own people? But again, the figures in the visuals were blurred, making it difficult to see the faces.

"Jihad ibadat hain...aur iss raah pe chalte huye jinko bhi shahdat milegi, use Allah tala jannat me panah bakshenge...usko phikr hi kya jab Malik ki barqaton se woh shaqs bahattar hooron ke sath la-fani waqt gujarega jannat me (Jihad is worship... and if someone falls on the path of jihad, the Almighty will provide him shelter in the heavens. He has nothing to worry as with Almighty's blessings, he will be spending an eternal life in company of seventy-two beautiful virgins.)"

The address ended with this note of promised bliss at the end of jihad for those who would perish. But the crowd was too young and charged up to even think of the aftermath at that point of time.

After the initial address, we were introduced to a Pakistan Army Officer, Major Rahamat Niyazi. The clean-shaven man in early thirties smartly turned up in military uniform. He was a stark contrast to the jihadist leaders, at least by appearance. He spoke with an air of authority that manifested from the official position he held with the government. He informed us that he would supervise our training that would be imparted by few retired soldiers of the Pakistan army. Something the Major mentioned that caught our fancy was the fact that once we successfully carried out jihad in the Indian side of Kashmir and returned, we would be inducted into regular

Pakistan army or the para military force. This was a big boost as a government job is what we all aspired for.

So, over the past twenty days, we have been imparted various skills in a field carved out of the slopes after clearing the forests some distance away from the madrasa. The so-called training area has a firing range, an obstacle course and classroom squad posts, where theoretical classes are held before the practical application.

We were initially given theoretical knowledge about few weapons like AK 47 Rifles, Browning 9mm pistols, Chinese grenades, Rocket Propelled Grenades (RPG) and improvised explosive device RDX. After each set of classes dedicated to particular weapons, we handled them to become comfortable with the feel of carrying them. We learnt how to break the weapons down to parts and then reassemble them to their original forms. The methods for carrying ammunition, filling them in the magazine, priming and hurling a grenade and safely carrying the plastic explosives before making an electronic circuit to detonate them by the help of wires and presser switches powered by batteries. Once we became confident, all these aspects were demonstrated practically by Major Niyazi and his team before we ourselves practiced firing, priming grenades and detonating small amounts of explosives. Pure adrenaline rush, I must say.

I pride myself in very fast unfolding of rifle parts and then assembling them back. While others used to take five to seven minutes, I could complete the entire process within two minutes. I realised that I was also very good with the obstacle course. Climbing stairs to reach a platform and then jump to hold a rope hanging about ten feet away for slithering down;

running over zigzag wooden planks; climbing a twenty-feet rugged wall with the help of a rope – these are few examples of the obstacles we were made to practice to negotiate and I excelled in all of these. We were also taught jungle survival skills like living off the land. It was mentioned that these would come handy when on few occasions, the oppressed Kashmiris would not be able to shelter us in their homes. Besides all these, we have received lessons on how to use hand held Motorola sets for communication and speak about serious issues encoded in lighter conversations. Finally, our session ended yesterday with lessons on map reading and the use of GPS.

The training sessions typically last for six to seven hours. Besides this we are expected to help with few daily chores in the madrasa like cleaning, collecting woods from the jungles etc. The hectic schedule had very little time for us to spend on our own. During one such rare recess, I had wandered off to an area behind the madrasa. We had been told not to venture there as it housed quarters of the senior leaders of the jihad council. They did not want to be disturbed by the trainees. I had actually spotted a very colourful kite flying down behind the madrasa building after being cut by another in a kite fight. Kite flying seemed to be a popular game this side and over the last few days, I have spotted many of these coloured paper pieces with their funny tails wagging behind them soaring high in the sky.

I suddenly heard human voices from an enclosure guarded by bamboo curtains. It appeared that someone was screaming but suppressed by layers of cloth. I tiptoed to a corner and peeped through. A man was hanging upside down from a tree, completely naked except for the undergarment. His sherwani lay crumpled some distance away. He was being spanked and hit by sticks and butts of rifles by people wearing camouflage dresses. Whenever they hit the guy, he screamed and then after that I was surprised to find that he started giggling.

"*Janab, thoda ahiste mariye*. Do you want to break my buttocks for real?" The man hanging upside down spoke with a comical expression. All men started laughing at this.

I must have stepped on a heap of fallen leaves that caused some susurration, which alerted the men. Before they could turn towards me, I was gone from the spot. I banged straight into Waqar Pathan, an important member of the leadership as I emerged in front of the madrasa building. He probably realised what I had seen. However, he smiled at me, ruffled my hair and admonished me in a playful tone.

"*Beta udhar jaana mana hain. Jo mukhbir pakde jaate hain unka ilaaj ka camp hain udhar.* (Son, it is prohibited to go that side. The spies who get caught are treated in a camp there.)"

I nodded and scurried past him with the kite in my hand. Well, it pays to be the best trainee in the camp. But this guy always tries to be physically close unnecessarily. He does not respect physical space and I abhor that. I have heard hushed rumours about him, but it is better to steer clear from both, the rumours and the subject of them.

We are often asked to tend to the senior jihadi leaders present in the camp. The commanders of terrorist groups like Jaish-e-Muhammad (JeM) and Lashkar-e-Taiba (LeT) frequent the camps and stay for a couple of days. They are very important leaders for the jihad and I heard that they travelled a lot in Pakistan and other countries, arranging finances and getting global support for our cause.

On one such occasion, I was told to carry food from the kitchen to a room on the third floor where Maulana Wajid was lodged. I carried a tray of roti, gosht and firni and climbed the stairs. The room was a stark contrast to the other lodgements in the madrasa. It was airy with all the windows open and facing the beautiful mountain ranges. The floor was covered with an intricately woven beautiful carpet. There was a television mounted on the wall and the bed was neatly done up. A small wooden dining table with four chairs was placed in one corner. The maulana was sitting on a cushioned sofa set and talking with Major Niyazi, who sat across him on a chair, wearing a maroon shirt and a pair of jeans. He puffed smoke from a cigarette as the two men continued their conversation.

"Major Sahab, Hukumat ko boliye budget badhane ke liye. PoK jyada bada jagah nahi hain ki nau jawanon ki line lag jayegi. Pakistan ke baaki ilakon se aur kuch aur Islamic mulkon se bande lane padhenge. (Major, tell the administration to increase the budget. PoK is not a big place that there would be uninterrupted supply of young men for jihad. So we have to bring youngsters from other parts of Pakistan and other countries)."

The maulana paused, looked out of the window and then spoke again.

"Aur hum logon ka bhi toh khayal rakhna padega. Koi rehnumaon ke bacche vilayat me padh rahe hain...kharcha aap ko malum hi hoga janab (And you have to look after us also... Many leaders' children are studying abroad and you must be aware of the expenses.)"

"Hum jante hain, maulana sahab, par yeh baatein aap muqddamon ke saamne pesh kare...aagle mahine ISI ke DG sahib ka daura hain...batayen unhe. (We know sir, but you must say these things to the top brass. Next month the DG of ISI will be visiting. You must apprise him about this.)"

I had kept the tray of food on the table and stood silently if they had any orders for me. Till then, neither had paid any attention to me. Then suddenly the maulana took notice of me. The middle-aged man had a scary disposition. He always wore an *aba* or sleeveless coat over the usual white gown and a white or checkered turban with a scarf hanging from either side of his head, with which he often wiped his greying beard. Through the black framed specs, a pair of cold intriguing eyes peered at me. The prying eyes had frozen the blood inside me and I found it difficult to move.

Following the gaze of the maulana, Major Niyazi found me standing as still as a prey seeing the predator just in front of him. He broke the silence by addressing me with some warmth in his voice that melted the ice and brought me back to my senses.

"Zahir...aap kya khana leke aaye hain? Thik hain mez par chod de use...aap jaa sakte hain. (Zahir, you have brought the food? Okay, leave it on the table and go.)"

I sprang out of the room and could hear the Major's voice behind me.

"He is a very bright student."

I was elated when day before yesterday, seeing me perform during the obstacle course, Major Niyazi patted me on the back and said, "*Bahut aage badhoge.* We are proud of youngsters like you."

Well, it is a fact that I have been better than all others in most of the disciplines.

Yesterday there was a sort of convocation during which Abu Musafir gave us the final pep talk.

"Allah ke rah chal kar agar aap me se kisiko shahdat bhi milti hain toh usse acchi maut nahi kisiko naseeb hoti hain. Jannat me aapko bahattar hoorain milegi aur jannat me sab se avval darza milega. Aur yaha ki phikr bhi na karein, kyunki agar aap logon ko kuch ho jaata hain toh aapke parivar walon ka khayal tanjeem rakkhega. Yeh aap logo ko Islam ke naam pe humara waida hain.

(While walking on the path of the Almighty, if anyone of you is martyred, then remember, no death is more glorious than this. You will be given seventy-two virgins in the afterlife to enjoy and you'll always be the privileged one in heaven. And do not worry about those you leave behind. They will be always taken care of by the jihadi regime. We promise you this in the name of Islam.)"

The hall inside the madrasa reverberated with claps and chants of *"Nara e Takbeer, Allahu Akbar! Nara-e-Takbeer, Allahu Akbar! Kashmir banega Pakistan! Kashmir banega Pakistan!'*

The convocation was graced by important jihadi leaders of whom we had heard or read about in newspapers.

We received ten thousand rupees in Indian currency to start with and were promised more cash once we cross over. It was said that our parents would be given one lakh rupees in Pakistan currency once we cross over into Indian territory. That is a huge amount of money. I felt good for my family staying back in the sleepy, small village of Dossud.

It's 1 a.m. now. It's so silent outside. I can only hear the sound of the river flowing down below. One more day before we embark on our mission across the border. Who knows what lies ahead of me in my river of life? My life has changed so much in the last one month. I have changed so much myself. I am calmer, my body has become leaner and muscular and I have become very alert about everything around me. This has been brought about by the arduous curriculum over the past twenty days. We have trained hard and slept not more than five hours in a day. We have been truly toughened up.

We have been divided into small groups of five to seven persons and each group has been assigned different points on the LoC for induction and separate handlers to guide us across.

I sign off today and will try to sleep now.

8

Zahir's Diary

Inside Indian Kashmir
20th May

For the last few days, we have travelled a lot. My group consisted of six of us, but now as I sit in the house of Amir Ali in this small village of *bakkarwal* (shepherds) writing my diary again, we are left with five in the group. We lost the youngest member of our team - Iqbal.

Iqbal was a bubbly chirping youngster whom I always felt, was too young to be pushed into this life. He was full of *josh* though. On the day of crossing, the Pakistan army men brought us to one of their check posts on the LoC. Then through jungle trails, our group reached a narrow mountain pass. We waited there for half an hour with bated breath, camouflaging ourselves in the vegetation. I could feel my blood run fast with excitement, because in a few moments, we all would be in an unknown, hostile territory.

The place was quiet, except for the faint roar of the river. Suddenly there was a whistling tone as if a bird called out. It was repeated twice. I looked over my head to catch the sight of the bird, but there was none. The Pakistan army soldier who was lying few yards from me crawled ahead few paces and raised himself on his knees. The bird whistled again in the same pitch, but now from very near. I realised it was done by this soldier. There was once again a sharper tweet from afar and then the guy spoke in a muffled voice, urging us to get on our feet and follow the trail going down from the pass.

As we stood up, we saw a man in Kashmiri dress peeping from behind a boulder on the trail and beckoning us to follow him. We jogged down the trail but he gestured us to walk slow. Once we reached him, he said that he was Masood, our guide till we reached deep inside the Kupwara district of Indian Kashmir.

We kept walking for the rest of the day till we halted for the night inside a temporary wooden shelter constructed by the shepherds to rest while grazing their cattle. Masood said we would be walking generally aligned to the LoC till reaching a suitable habitation to make our base for the next few days. We cooked the dry ration we carried and slept keeping one person as a sentry and relieving him after every two hours by another.

The next day, we commenced our journey. Iqbal was in full gusto. He spoke loudly in excitement, in spite of Masood refraining him from doing so. He mentioned several times how lucky he was that he got this chance to serve the Almighty and would carry out jihad fiercely in Kashmir. He would not mind even if he had to carry out *fidayeen* attacks on Indian security forces.

I laughed within myself and wondered if this boy even knew the meaning of what he was rattling out. No wonder the brain washing by the jihadi leaders had been very effective.

We reached a beautiful valley and halted for lunch that comprised of roti and khajoor. The green valley had pine and rhododendron trees rolling up on the slope of the hills on one side and a crystal clear stream meandering down on the other. It cascaded down a rock face and formed a pool before flowing down. The channel was not visible from the spot where we had halted as it ran a little downwards. We could hear the cackling sound of the water over the pebbles and see beautiful butterflies fluttering their wings in a swarm over the orchids strewn around the bank of the rivulet. The scene was so divine that all of us were mesmerised and literally had forgotten about the perils that lay in every inch of this beautiful piece of land.

Masood had warned us not to stray from the group but Iqbal, as usual charged by his adrenaline, scooted towards the fountain to take a bath. Masood half-heartedly tried to restrain him, but before he could physically stop him, he had vanished below the raised spur forming the bank of the stream.

Suddenly, there was a deafening sound caused by an explosion and a loud shriek. It was so instantaneous and out of the place that we froze in alarm for moments. Then as we got up to dash for the source of the sound, Masood shouted at us and started running in the opposite direction urging us to follow him.

"Bhai Iqbal ko kuch hua hai (Brother, something has happened to Iqbal)," I pleaded with him.

Without stopping, he responded that probably he had stepped on a mine laid by the Indian security forces and soon they would come looking hearing the explosion. And if we stayed, we could all get killed or captured.

We paced to enter a dense forested area with Masood. Finally, he stopped after almost thirty minutes of frantic running and halted behind a big boulder. Panting for breath, he told us that we needed to be very stealthy and discrete as danger lay in every nook and corner in this territory.

Maqbool, another youth in our group demanded angrily why Masood had not stopped Iqbal.

"*Pakistan Fauj ka dimaag kharab ho gaya hai ki aise bacchon ko itna jokhim wale kaam pe lagate hain. Uske saath jo huwa aaj nahi toh kal hona hi tha aur Allah na kare aap sab ko uska anjam bhugatna padta.* (The Pakistan army has gone mad that they are sending kids for such risky jobs. What happened to him was inevitable, and would have happened today or tomorrow. God forbid, you all would have to face the consequences.)" Masood shrugged his shoulders in a gesture of helplessness.

I took a good look at him. It occurred to me that people like Masood had no conscience left anymore and did whatever he was doing only for money. I felt he had purposefully got rid of Iqbal. He knew about the minefield and yet chose that valley to halt. I shall have to be careful with this man.

In the evening, we had reached this village and lodged with Amir Ali for the night. Let's see how things shape up over the next few days.

9

The Messiah from the other side

Captain Zeenat paused after reading till this point and looked at Karim. The next account of Zahir in the diary started almost two months later. She asked about what transpired in between and how Karim got into the scheme of Zahir's agenda.

"Zahir, I guess, caught up with settling down and pursuing his agenda with full devotion, stopped writing the diary for some time. However, I will pick up from here as it was at this point where my life became stringed with Zahir's and my initiation into jihad took place," Karim explained and continued narrating the events of his life.

So, it was a pleasant day in the month of May. Karim had played a game of cricket and returned home in the afternoon to find a young man of his age sitting in the front room of their house. His father introduced the young man to him and said that he had come from the other side and would stay with the family for a few days.

Amanullah, Karim's father was a peace loving, religious and god-fearing man. He had been already shown the video clips of the so-called torture of Kashmiris by the Indian security forces and had agreed to shelter Zahir in their house, however with a condition that there should not be any trouble inside the premises of his quaint residence. The fact that people like Amanullah were typically ignorant about the world outside made it easy for the jihadis to manipulate and convince for shelter, refuge and other assistance in name of jihad. Zahir started sharing Karim's room and gradually began initiating the latter on the path of jihad.

It was like a chain reaction. One contact to another got many absorbed into the idea of the insurgency, exploiting the orthodoxy of the Kashmiris. Karim mentioned that after reading the literature that Zahir was carrying, he felt that till Kashmir was not ceded from the Indian mainland, a Hindu majority nation, there was no hope for the Muslims to live with dignity. The hatred, anger and contempt for other faiths were so deeply seeded in those manuals and articles that people like him, who had very little exposure to the outside world, would become blindly obsessed with the idea of jihad.

"We had hardly come across any non-Muslim persons in our village and the neighborhood, which has been our world. So, the mere concept of other religious practices was very contemptuous for us, especially if it was propagated to be causing the oppression of Islam," Karim remarked apologetically.

"Hmm...we have seen the very same pattern all across the valley. Simple and innocent youths being brainwashed. But how did your training take place in this village?" Col Manav asked with his eyes reflecting pity and empathy for the injured youngster lying in front of him.

Karim mentioned that it was not possible to receive training the way Zahir had received, but he was exposed to the rifles and other arms. Zahir had said that he would be doing on the job training, which meant participating in live operations against the Indian security forces.

Zahir had carried an AK-47, sixty bullets and two grenades when he had stepped inside the household. He had demonstrated the use of those weapons and then promised Karim he'd show him other weapons once he received the consignment.

After a few days, one fine morning, Zahir had asked Karim to accompany him. He had a Motorola walkie-talkie through which he used to communicate with others who had crossed over with him and were lodged at other villages. They walked uphill till they reached the top of a crest line. Zahir took out his walkie-talkie and spoke to people from the Balakote training camp. The Pakistanis had their radio signal relay stations established near the LoC on their side and through those, these small range devices could transmit and receive signals over longer distances.

Karim said the conversation was very casual, making no sense to him, but he had later learnt that there was useful information hidden in them to evade the Indian security forces who scanned all frequencies to intercept communication between militants. Karim explained with an example:

Zahir: *Salam alaikum Bhai Jaan...* (Greetings Brother)

The other side: *Alaikum Salam, Aur sab khairiyat?* (Greetings Brother, All ok?

Zahir: *Bilkool janab, Allah ka shukr hain...* (Yes sir, by the grace of the Almighty.)

The other side: *Bahut sardi hain...Bade Taya ke liye adhe darjan dibba ankhon ka marham bhejha hoon aur chir ka tel, dono hathon me malish karna roj ek dafa...* (It's very cold. Have sent half a dozen bottles of eye lotion for the elder uncle and also pine oil...massage on both of his arms once daily.)

Zahir: *Ji Bhai sahab*

The other side: *Aur cricket bahut khelte ho aajkal, boundary marte ho Afridi ki tarah aur hatrick bhi lete ho Waqar jaisa... bilkool avval khilari ban gaye ho...ha ha ha...* (And you play cricket a lot nowadays...you have been hitting boundaries like Afridi and taking hat tricks like Waqar a lot. You have become the number one player.)

Zahir: *Bas Bhai Sahab dua hai...time nikalna hai* (By God's grace Brother...have to take out time.)

The other side: *Chalo, Khayal rakhna aur khat likhna Abbu ke liye exam ke turant baad. Kuch paise bhejhe hain Chacha jaan ke haath mil jayega...* (Ok see you. take care and write a letter to father immediately after the exams. Have sent some money too with uncle, you will get it.)

Zahir: *Ji jaroor. Bahut padhai karni hain, Intehan khatm hote he khabar bhejhta hoon.* (Sure. Have to study a lot. Will catch up after the exams.)

This was a seemingly normal conversation between two individuals even if they were militants, who might be related and sharing casual pleasantries. But there was a six-figure grid reference hidden in it... 'half a dozen' was 6, 'both of his arms' was 2, 'once' was 1, 'boundary' meant 4, 'hat trick' a 3 and 'number one' was 1. Zahir had then explained that 621 431 was the grid reference on the map where some consignment would be available.

Karim's child-like face glowed in spite of the fragile state of his health.

Karim had accompanied Zahir as he plotted the position on a map and with the help of a GPS, reached the spot after a walk of about one hour. It was deep inside a jungle and there was no habitat around. He kept scanning the area like a hawk would look for a prey from the air. Then he had pointed out a small green piece of cloth tied across the twig of a mulberry tree.

"Here it is," Zahir spoke through his heavy breathing caused by the labour of treading on the terrain.

The cloth was so insignificant and merged so deviously with the foliage that it would not be possible for a normal man to pick up. There were faint marks of shovel having been used on the ground under the tree. Zahir started to move the soil from the spot with bare hands and asked Karim to help. He was quick. Not much of effort was required and soon the upper surface of a wooden chest emerged from the dugout soil. Both of them displaced some more soil from the periphery and heaved the box out of the earth. It was about five feet in length. Zahir opened the chest and there was a green colored tube, which he explained to Karim, was a Rocket Propelled Grenade Launcher tube. The box also contained ammunition to be fired from the weapon.

As Karim looked bewildered at the discovery, Zahir placed it on his shoulder and took an aim at the nearest ridge line.

He added that this weapon could be fired at any armoured car like bullet-proof vehicles or Mine Protected Vehicles (MPVs) and inflict heavy casualty on the passengers. The warhead in the cartridge was a high explosive anti-tank (HEAT) grade ammo which exploded on impact with the body of the vehicle. It would pierce the armour, topple the car and even blow up a vehicle if hit at the fuel tank. He smiled at a petrified Karim and allowed him to have a feel of the weapon.

Zahir mentioned zealously that with the RPG, he would blow away the armoured patrol vehicles of the Indian Army known as Caspir. They had been shown the pictures and video clips of these vehicles in the Balakote camp.

Karim took a close look at the dangerous looking thing. It had markings of the Pakistan army engraved on the surface and weighed about six to seven kgs. It was very comfortable resting on the shoulder and had a wooden handle to hold by hand and take aim. After the initial hesitation the slender piece of inflicting devastation gave a high to a novice like Karim.

But that was not all. There was another item packed in a polythene bag. It contained a light yellowish rubbery substance. Zahir held the RDX, around one kilogram in mass, on his palms delicately and laughed hysterically staring at it with frenzied eyes. The excitement oozed beads of perspiration on his forehead, defying the chill in the air of the fast-approaching evening.

"Qayamat Karim bhai...Qayamat! Itna sa cheez do se teen buson ko uda sakta hain...ek pakka pul ko bi deh dega. (Dangerous this is, Karim bhai! This much of this material can blow up two to three buses...can even destroy a concrete bridge!")

Having collected all these items, they returned to Karim's place. It was dark by then and the load carrying silhouettes were not noticed by anyone. People in the villages retired early and hardly stayed out of their houses at night. Karim led Zahir to the sheep pen behind their house. There was a small, dry well dug on the ground, about three feet in depth and five feet in width with a latched cover, where during summers water was stored for the sheep. Zahir placed the weapon, ammunition and the explosive carefully inside the cavity and locked the door on the ground.

10

Zahir and Karim: the plan and the people

"Is this the sheep pen?" Col Manav walked up to the window on the southern wall of the room and pointed down at a mud walled structure with an asbestos roof.

Karim nodded in agreement.

"So, what happened after that? Did you people carry out any operations with the shipment Zahir received?" Col Manav asked while looking out at the distant lines of oaks, birches and deodars gradually ascending to merge with the dark green ridgeline guarding the horizon.

Karim continued his story. The next few days were spent in planning the first operation against the Indian security forces by Zahir and his team. Zahir used to go out often and meet others who had crossed over with him and were staying in other villages. Karim had accompanied him on a couple of occasions, but he was not allowed to be a part of the discussion.

During these voyages to meet with the accomplices, Karim and Zahir had to take shelter at random villagers' houses for the night. While few were happy to host them, most seemed like they were extending the hospitality under compulsion and fear.

"Akhir masla kya hai? Yahan toh log bahut jyada khush nahi dikhte humhe dekhkar...

(What is the issue after all? Here people do not look very happy seeing us,)" Zahir had asked a man tending to his apricot farms in a village.

He informed that the ongoing turmoil in the Kashmir valley had taken a toll on the people. They were largely worn out and tired of the mindless violence continuing for so long. It had affected the economy, education and development of the Kashmiri people severely.

"*Par azadi?* Don't you people want freedom from the Indian rule?"

"Who sab amir daulat shumar logon ke liye hain bhaijaan... Garibon ko do waqt ki roti, sukoon, bacchon ki salamati aur chain ki neend chahiye. (All that is for rich and prosperous people, brother. Poor people want two square meals, solace, the wellbeing of their children and peaceful sleep at night.)"

As the man had hurried back with his small produce towards his house, Zahir kept staring at the retreating man with creases forming on his forehead.

The plan for the sabotage had been worked out. Zahir had shifted the RPG and the RDX to a hiding place in the jungle nearby the Sopore-Kupwara highway. They would be used in the night and the action would be taking place in the wee hours of the morning.

After gathering intelligence about movement of the army coloumns in the area, Zahir and his team members had dispersed to meet after the midnight on the day of the planned assault at a designated place. Karim accompanied Zahir to a village near the highway for seeking shelter for the night. They had their rifles and ammunition under their phiran and knocked at a modest dwelling located at the approach to the village. The sun had settled behind the distant hills for the day and the lush farmlands expanding till the faraway tree lines of the jungle wore a deserted look as the twilight smeared everything with darkening shades layer after layer.

The door was opened by an old man and a little boy. The old man stared at them with blank cataract laden eyes while the kid, who was around seven or eight years old bore an expression of innocence and alarm. Zahir greeted the old man and requested for refuge for the night.

"*Hum aap logon ko panah nahi de sakte hain. Beshaq aap goli mar dijiye ham logon ko. Meherbani karke chale jaiye* (We can't provide you shelter. If you want, you can kill us. Please go away from here.)"

The old man had not even bothered to ask who they were.

Zahir was shocked. He was apologetic, but also wanted to know the reason behind such a scornful attitude of the old man.

The old man did not budge. He said he had seen enough in his lifetime, and the few days he had, he would like to look after his grandson and the daughter-in-law well.

Karim proffered a bundle of Indian currency, that Zahir had given him to keep, to the old man so that he would be tempted to give them refuge for the night. But the old man lost his cool. He asked the boy to go inside and slammed the door behind him. The rusted bolts squeaked in protest and startled a squirrel that was merrily gnawing on some fallen figs on the grounds nearby. It scooted and disappeared into a nearby bush. The man held Karim by his collar and dragged his face close to his.

"*Aap jaise pehle bhi bahut aaye. Hum garib hain par in napaak paison se koi matlab nahi hume...in paison se kya aap mere bete ko wapas kar sakte ho?* (Many people like you had come earlier. We are poor, but we do not want this sinful money. Can this money get my son back?)"

There was pain and fury in his eyes as his bearded wrinkled face convoluted in disgust.

He then suddenly let Karim go. Karim was too startled to react. He wiped his face with the back of the sleeve of his phiran which had been moistened by the spittle of the old man.

The old man then looked away from them and continued. He narrated how five years earlier, guys like them had come to stay in this household. They called themselves 'Mujahid', fighting the cause of Islam. They were carrying out jihad and encouraged his only son to join their ranks. His son had refused and wanted to live a peaceful life by running his small grocery shop. After a few days, one evening, the Mujahids picked up the young man from his shop and hung him in the nearby jungle, suspecting him of being a spy for the army.

"The old man broke down mentioning that his son was not a traitor or spy, but wanted to live a simple, happy life with his family.

"Yeh hain aap logon ka jihad?" Howling with pain the old man demanded if Jihad meant harassing innocent people, killing them and getting them killed. He added that in every

house in the village, someone or other had been killed in this so called jihad. Moreover, people like Zahir and Karim would always fetch police behind their trails, which would lead to further harassment for the villagers in the name of interrogations. The simple villagers had no relief from either side.

As the old man went back inside his home, Zahir and Karim left the spot and headed towards the jungle. The eerie silence between them was broken by Zahir, who said that they would be spending the night in the jungle.

11

The first bang

The pain on Karim's eyes was very much visible as he continued to narrate his experiences with militancy. It showed in his strained expressions as if the man had to exert himself to recount those days of violence and bloodshed; every bit of which he seemed to repent.

There was an abandoned *dhok* or shelter built by the shepherds to rest inside the jungle. They waited there till midnight. Zahir tried to shake off the mellowing effect that the words of the old man had cast upon them.

"Karim, hum Allah ke sipahi hain...aur hume yeh padhaya gaya ki Islam ke dushmonon ke khilaf jung hi jihad hain...yeh awam musalmano ke khilaf hain...humare majhab ke khilaf hain. Kuch masoom logon ki kurbani is jihad ke raah me deni padegi...par Kashmiriyon ko hum azadi dilayenge in kafiron se... (Karim, we are the soldiers of the Almighty and we have been taught that to fight against the enemies of Islam is Jihad. This country is against the Muslims. It is anti-Islam. It's true that few innocent people would be sacrificed for this cause, but we will liberate Kashmiris from the infidels."

Karim too had tried to charge himself up by these words. He had never had any infidel friend. The only ones he had seen were the army people who used to patrol the areas in and around his village. He had heard though that there were many Hindus in Kashmir earlier who had been driven away to other parts of India. Kashmir was meant for Muslims only. But then he pondered for a while if there were Muslims in other parts of India too? Like in Delhi, Bombay, etc.

Yes, why not? The great actors in Hindi films like Shahrukh Khan, Salman Khan and Amir Khan. They were his favourites. But then, how could they stay in Bombay and live happily? Nobody threw them out from there. He brushed away these uncomfortable thoughts keeping them for Zahir bhai to explain later. He was only bothered about Kashmir as of now.

He had dozed off and was startled out of his sleep by the shrill hooting of a night bird. Zahir, who had stayed awake and alert, stood up and signaled him to follow. They carried the packet of explosives and the RPG and walked for half an hour till they reached the highway. The undulating road lay like a black ribbon dimly lit by the moon. It was past midnight and there were no traffic or human presence on the road. As decided earlier, six more jihadis had assembled at that spot. Two of them had come with Zahir from Pakistan and four were local recruits like Karim. They all carried AK-47 rifles.

The stretch of the road had been selected after deliberate recce. The road was being tarmacked there and the tar from the top had been scraped off baring the soil underneath. There was a dense pocket of vegetation on one side and an untended apple orchard on the other side of the road; both having a vantage effect over the road owing to the slightly raised grounds on which they were situated. The spot provided good cover and a free run to the jungles on either side.

Under instructions from Zahir, four men started digging the soft soil on the road to create a cavity. Four others stood guard as look out sentries on the road and the surrounding grounds. Zahir cautiously took out the explosive from his satchel and put it in a big stainless steel watering pot used in gardening after removing the soft muslin cloth. Karim took a close look at it. So harmless it looked, just like a bar of soap or cheese. The container already had some powdery substance and once the explosive was well fitted inside, Zahir poured some more of the powder on top of it. That was gunpowder, he explained in a hushed voice. The lid of the pot was then closed tightly. Two electric wires, naked at the end and joined together were inserted through the nozzle so that they could touch the body of the explosive. The wires were then stretched till five hundred metres from the road and covered with the loose soil dug out earlier. Two large battery cells were placed in a bamboo sheath tied across the slender trunk of a tree concealed by the foliage. The other end of the wires were then connected with the upper battery terminals. Another pair of wires were connected with the lower terminals and the far end of the same were then fitted to a presser switch used in houses for operating light bulbs. Thus a circuit was completed. The switch laid approximately 750 metres away from the place where the explosive had been placed. The pit on the road was then covered up and any tell-tale signs of human intervention on that spot were smoothened out. The trap was set.

This procedure had taken about an hour and finally when all the people of the group had taken positions reasonably away from the road so that they would not be affected by the blast, it was thirty minutes past three in the morning. Zahir's commands were simple and crisp. As per the sources of information, around four in the morning, a small army convoy would be moving towards Sopore from Kupwara. They would be expected to reach the spot in forty-five minutes. Once the third vehicle of the convoy consisting of five or six vehicles crossed the place where the explosive had been placed, Zahir would activate the circuit and the powerful explosive would go off. Simultaneously, the group deployed in pairs and scattered inside the jungles would fire towards the convoy. The confusion would prevail for some time and after three minutes of firing, the group would disengage and disappear into the deeper jungles.

One of the men in the group asked Zahir that if they were sitting astride the road and firing, they could be firing at each other while aiming at the convoy. Zahir smiled and replied that they needed to stagger while deploying and form a 'V' with the place of the explosive as an imaginary vortex so that they fired in a tangent, without hitting each other.

Karim and Zahir sat as a pair. The minutes seemed like hours and Karim had this urge of quitting and running away. He was not sure if he was ready for such a macabre experience. One half of him wanted to give up and the other half still managed to keep him motivated for the sake of the noble cause, the holy war against infidels.

Zahir had probably sensed Karim's restlessness. He patted Karim on his back and whispered, "This is the Almighty's command."

Karim had lost count of the minutes and hours when suddenly the stretch of the road ahead got illuminated by a faint beam of light. It was the headlight of an approaching vehicle. It was 5 a.m. in the morning and yet the sky had remained shrouded by the veil of the retreating night's darkness. Zahir switched on the Motorola walkie-talkie set and spoke softly "*Taiyar?* Ready, my friends?" Then again, there were moments of strained silence. Karim stared at the road focusing on the spot where the explosive had been planted. The first vehicle was an Army Maruti Gypsy. It crossed the spot and rolled ahead. But then there were no other vehicles behind it. The car stopped fifty metres ahead of the spot and there was the sound of the door being opened and banged shut. Someone had stepped out of the car. Karim and Zahir looked at each other in consternation. Zahir instructed all to hold fire on the walkie talkie. Karim thought he heard someone say, *"Aane do, Sahab ji."* He froze with horror. He was certain that they had got a whiff of the trap and would be coming for them. He had stood up, but Zahir caught him by his arm and pulled him down. He gestured at Karim to keep quiet. They could hear faint footsteps from that distance. A good five minutes elapsed. Then three things happened one after another.

There was a sound of a rifle being cocked, making Zahir and Karim dive flat on the ground; doors of the vehicle opened and closed for a second time and a broad high beam of light gradually approached the ambush spot.

Zahir heaved a sigh of relief and got back to his haunches, nudging Karim to do so as well. As the Gypsy's engine growled softly and it started moving, an army truck arrived at the scene. Probably the column had got too stretched and the leading vehicle had stopped for the others to close in. The first truck passed and in seconds, the next one arrived at the spot.

Click.

The sound was faint, yet distinct. Zahir had pressed on the switch.

And then there was mayhem.

It felt as if thunder had struck the ground just beside them. Karim and Zahir were both picked up from the ground and flung on opposite directions from each other. In spite of the impact, Karim could observe from the corner of his eyes that the 7.5 ton army truck was literally in the air before it fell on the farther side of the road. He could not imagine what would remain of the vehicle. The one following the blown away truck had also been thrown away from the road to one side, though the strength of the impact was lesser. As Karim fell on the ground, he could feel the shock wave actually getting transmitted under him in ripples. His eyes were blinded from the flash he had seen and the ears ringed with tinnitus from the sound of the explosion.

"Qahr e qayamat," Karim kept praying to god, thinking through the daze that this was far more dangerous than what had been claimed by Zahir. His vision and hearing cleared as he could see Zahir already on his feet and the uncanny, immediate, momentary calm post the big bang was broken by Zahir shouting at him, "Fire Karim... fire!"

Karim could also hear the shouting of the soldiers from the spot. He wondered how many had perished. His arms felt heavy. Yet he managed the strength to pick up his rifle and started firing indiscriminately. He could now hear firing from the other spots also, where the members of the group had recovered from the shock and launched their attack.

As if this was not enough, to utter trepidation of Karim, Zahir had placed the RPG on his shoulder and aimed it at the fifth vehicle of the convoy, a 2.5 ton truck and pressed the trigger. With a loud bang, the rocket propelled ammunition left the muzzle and scooted for the target at lightning speed. But the truck was probably beyond the hitting range and the rocket exploded before reaching it in the air, splattering the ground with its fragments and shrapnel which could have hit soldiers taking guard behind the contours of the ground. However, it definitely added to the element of shock.

Three minutes had elapsed and the firing had stopped. Zahir discarded the RPG in the nearby ditch as it would be difficult to run with it and signaled Karim to run along with him. Suddenly there were flurry of bullets flying over their heads, right and left. The soldiers had gained control after the initial thaw and started firing at them. Each bullet hissed sharply like a cruel serpent as they pierced the morning air, desperately seeking to strike human flesh.

Karim took shelter behind a tree and froze. He had completely run out of focus, not knowing what to do next. He was pulled out of the stalemate by Zahir with a slap on his face, and then as if in a reflex to Zahir's action, he started running. The firing, yelling and the commotion dwindled away behind them and soon they found themselves in the dhok they had used to rest temporarily earlier in the evening.

The walkie-talkie cackled. *"Bhaijan... Bilawal aur Arshad ko goli lag gayi...unhe chodna para...shayad zinda nahi hain*

(Brother, Bilawal and Arshad have been hit. We had to leave them. Probably they are no more.)"

Bilawal and Arshad were two local Kashmiri youths who had joined the ranks like Karim.

"Allah unke shahdat qabul karenge...Insha Allah. (The Almighty will accept their martyrdom.)"

Zahir then had taken out a small mobile phone from his trouser pocket and dialed a number.

"*Barat khatam.* (Marriage party finished.)"

"Shabash. Naaz hain aap par...Alhamdulillah. Jihad Zindabad (Well done. We are proud of you. God be thanked. Long live the holy war.)" A voice had replied from the other side.

Karim and Zahir kept moving the whole day cross country, avoiding villages and human population. Zahir carried a small transistor which he had switched on during a brief halt in an open place so that it could catch the signal. The news being broadcasted by All India Radio, Srinagar mentioned the incident. Hijbul Mujahideen had claimed responsibility of the attack on the Army convoy on the Sopore-Kupwara road. Four soldiers had been martyred, three vehicles damaged and two terrorists killed by the army.

Zahir listened to the news and then nodded his head several times. *"Hindustan ke fauj shahid aur humare sathi maare gaye? Yeh bulletin toh Srinagar se pesh kiya jaa raha hain, phir kya Kashmir ke log is Jihad ke saath nahi hain?* (Indian Army soldiers have been martyred and our brothers have been killed? This bulletin is being presented from Srinagar, then are the people of Kashmir not supporting this jihad?)"

Karim was too overwhelmed to respond. The enormity of the incident had started to sink in. They resumed their journey. They were moving towards the north-eastern direction and Zahir mentioned that they would be hiding around the Bandipora town for the next few days. Arrangements had been made by people from Balakote. It was dangerous to be in the Sopore or the Kupwara area as the army would carry out terrorist hunting operations. Karim, who actually wanted to go back to his home, had no other option but to accompany Zahir. Had it not been for the affection and bonding they shared, Karim would have deserted Zahir and headed back to his village.

Karim paused after narrating the story this far. His face showed the strain of reminiscing the fearful days. Col Manav, an experienced soldier, could understand well that these youths had been misled to take part in these dangerous games which were beyond their capabilities to handle.

Zeenat enquired if Zahir's diary commenced again from this point, but Manav did not want to pressurize Karim anymore. They took leave for the day and informed him that the session would continue over the following few days.

12

Zeenat and her recurring nightmare

"*Bemanono...mat jaiye bahaar! (Bro-in-law, no...don't go out side.)*"

"Ehsaan beta, abhi golibari shuru ho jayegi, ruuk jao thodi der... (*Ehsaan, son, the firing will start any moment...wait for some time.)*"

"Janwar maare jayenge Abbu... ek minute ka kaam hain. (*The animals will die. I will be back in a minute.)*"

The main door of the house closed behind Ehsaan loudly as he dashed out of the house. Immediately there were rattling sounds of fire outside and a loud shriek. The door opened, blown apart by furious winds, and the bloodied figure of Ehsaan walked in before slumping on the floor in a pool of blood. The house filled with hysteric cries from all the members who were waiting anxiously for Ehsaan to return safely. Suddenly, the scene plunged into darkness.

Zeenat sprang up from her sleeping posture, panting heavily. The beads of perspiration on her forehead glistened like tiny pearls reflecting in the faint light of the night lamp. She took few moments to realise where she was and as gradually the effect of the nightmare started receding, she eased. She took a gulp of water from the bottle kept beside her bed on the peg table and splashed water on her face. Though the water was ice cold, it soothed her. She switched on the bedroom lights and sat on the bed inhaling and exhaling deeply to relax her strained nerves. It would take some time for her to fall asleep again.

She was listening to the recording of Karim's accounts before going to sleep. It was a practice in her job to record important conversations. No doubt the horrific acts of terror narrated by Karim had triggered the nightmare. The scenes recurred in her dreams as the trauma was too deep to be cleansed forever. Her mind could not help but travel once again to those days she had left behind seven years back. Eventful days in the life of a final year college student.

Her final year exams of graduation were over and Zeenat had just returned home in the outskirts of Srinagar a couple of days earlier. She had been studying in a college in Srinagar and stayed in a hostel there. She was a good student and was certain of getting a first class. She was figuring out a way to convince her parents to let her go to Delhi for pursuing a master's degree in English Literature. Also, Delhi would offer her an option to play basketball for the university team and who knew, she could even be selected for the national squad!

With these dreams, she had returned to her ancestral house in the village, to be pampered by her parents and sisters. Her elder sister Nusrat and her husband Ehsaan had come over to stay with them for a few days. The house resonated with the laughter of the sisters, Zeenat and Rubayat, who took turns in pulling the legs of their beloved bro-in-law and the non-stop chattering of Mir, the three-year-old son of Nusrat and Ehsaan.

Ehsaan owned a huge apple orchard inherited from his father in Awantipora and also did trading of garments from Jammu and Punjab. He was a jovial, energetic and handsome young man.

The day Zeenat had returned to her village, she had seen two unknown youths sitting on a bench in front of a local shop sipping tea. She knew most of the people from her village and could tell by glancing at them that they were strangers. Lanky, bearded youths who had looked at her and smiled for no reason. It was true that Zeenat was quite good looking and possessed a lithe figure of an athlete, but something about the disposition of those guys had caused a sense of unknown trepidation in her mind. At the same time, the attention received from these young men had taken her mind back to someone in Srinagar who shied away from saying something to her. She had forced out the sense of alien fear and blushed thinking about her college mate who had stirred the lovelorn heart for the first time in her life.

As she had approached her gated house dragging her trolley suitcase, the dense pink blossoms of the bougainvillea swayed merrily in the afternoon breeze to greet her. This tree had been planted by Zeenat a few years back on a corner of the small garden in front of the house, and every spring, the blooms grew more plentiful. It instantly buoyed her spirits and the glee of meeting her folks grew by several shades of colours displayed in her tiny garden.

Days passed. Then one afternoon, there was an announcement from the mosque of the village that the Army had cordoned off the village as there were suspected militants holed up in a house inside. Villagers were requested to keep calm and cooperate with the soldiers who would check for any suspicious persons in the village.

This announcement was followed by the blaring of the microphones of the Army people. They announced that they would be going from house to house in search of a couple of men who had infiltrated from Pakistan and were hiding in the village. They requested the villagers to stay inside their houses. Having studied in Srinagar, Zeenat was not new to these kind of operations by the Army or police. She knew that if they all stayed inside, there would not be anything to be afraid of.

She asked her parents if they had spotted two youths in the village whom she had seen the day she had returned from the hostel. Though her parents intimated that they did not know about any strangers coming to anybody's home in the village, Zeenat had a hunch that it had to be them. Theirs was a big habitat with more than hundred houses located on the rolling folds of the valley, and it would not be an easy task to find the two youths hidden in somebody's house.

At this point, suddenly there was a loud bleating of the sheep outside the house. The flock consisting of five sheep remained outside the house, roaming in the backyard, especially when they were not being grazed in the distant fields. They were put into the pen after the last light. Zeenat, who had been well acquainted with the ways of the animals knew that the sheep called out due to some disturbance or interference in their peaceful munching. She had opened the window that faced the back of the house in one of the bedrooms and had found several stones lying on the ground. Somebody had thrown stones at them, making them cry out.

Before she could react, Ehsaan, not heeding to the pleas of the others, had gone out of the front door to put the animals inside the pen. Zeenat kept a watch on him from the window as he assembled the animals and herded them towards the pen located on the eastern flank of the house.

After a minute, Zeenat was shocked to find a man standing up from behind the periphery wall of their house and shoot a few bullets towards the approach road to the village that divided the settlement into two parts. It was one of the strangers whom Zeenat had encountered the other day. So her hunch had not been wrong. After shooting, the man disappeared behind the wall, but the firing had attracted the attention of the security forces, who instantly fired back in that direction. Before Zeenat shrieked and closed the window in a flash, she saw Ehsaan slumping down on the ground. She was too petrified to react. She was startled back to her senses once she heard loud bangs on the door. From the room, she could see a bloodied Ehsaan dropping down on the floor.

The security forces had cordoned off their house and had very quickly understood that they had been tricked by the devious militants. They had fired from the backyard of the Mirza household, leading the security personnel to believe they were hidden in that house. The crossfire had caught Ehsaan in its path and fatally injured him. He had succumbed almost instantly. In this melee, the militants had tried to sneak out of the village.

The loss was irreplaceable. Ehsaan had passed away for no fault of his. It was the clever and dastardly ploy of the militants who never hesitated to utilise the innocent people for their cause. Both the militants had been eliminated though, and since then, Zeenat's hatred for these people had grown manifold. Had she not seen what happened, it would have led her to put the blame on the security forces for the death of her brother-in-law.

So when the army authorities had reached out to the family, providing an employment to the widow of late Ehsaan, it was Zeenat who volunteered in place of her elder sister to join the Indian Army. She was groomed in one of the cantonments by officials before appearing in the pre-requisite exams. She had succeeded in the first attempt and after a successful one-year training with some of the best youths from across the country, she had earned her commission as a lieutenant in the Indian Army.

Zeenat looked at the photo hanging on the wall where she was receiving the gold medal for being the best lady cadet in her batch in the Officers Training Academy during the passing out parade. As her senses migrated back to the quaint precincts of her quarter, her eyes shifted from one frame to another on the wall; a group of young lady officers standing wearing the stars on the shoulders, just after their commissioning; Lt Zeenat with her parents and sister at the high tea organized by the Army soon after the passing out parade; a smiling Capt Zeenat, carrying a parachute on her back, flashing a victory sign just before jumping off an air force transporter plane from an altitude of 14,000 feet.

What a life it had been since then!

Chapter 13
The emerging truth and Project Goodwill

The next day, Col Manav and Capt Zeenat joined Karim for a hearty breakfast at his place.

Karim informed them that Zahir's diary resumed with the story of Aliah, but there were a few interesting incidents during their wandering off days that had led Zahir to Aliah. Karim continued his narration.

Continuing with the exodus from Sopore area immediately after the ambush on the Army convoy, Zahir moved cross country by reading a map and plotting waypoints on the GPS. Initially they had moved down south along the highway and crossed the Jhelum river over a temporary bridge constructed by locals at a narrow stretch of the river. Once they reached the other side, they had continued their north easterly journey, keeping the Sopore-Bandipora road and the Wular lake to the east. They followed the alignment of the road and marched through the jungles just below the crest line, as the upstream journey along the lake would lead them to Bandipora.

They walked for two days and in spite of the fear of being pursued, Karim could not help but appreciate the terrain they were marching on. They gained altitude as they kept closing on Bandipora. The upper crests of the ridgeline were covered with snow that shone like gold by the rays of the early morning sun and sizzled like a necklace in the silvery radiance of the moonlit night. At places, they could see the vast blue expanse of the Wular Lake with the waves rippling on its shores. The surface of the lake mirrored the puffy cotton-ball clouds, wandering as vagrantly as they were, and the snow-clad peaks looming with extended arms to embrace the aquamarine expanse from all sides.

When they had covered half the distance to their destination, they came across a small village, Sakhipora, located on the lower altitudes. An old woman was sitting in the courtyard, doing some household chores. They greeted the old woman and tried to strike a conversation. The woman was not cordial and asked them if they were Mujahids. Zahir affirmed her notion and requested for a night stay. They badly needed a warm cooked meal and uninterrupted sleep in a walled enclosure. These areas were much colder than the lower valleys of Sopore and Kupwara.

The woman agreed to give them some food but sternly refused any accommodation. The story was same as of the old man they had encountered near Sopore two days back.

"*Yeh raahen aap chod de. Kuch nahi hasil honewala hain isse...naujawan ho aap log kuch sahi kaam karo...budhape me Ma Baap ka sahara bano.* (Leave this path you are walking on! You will gain nothing by this. You people are young; do something good and try to become the support for your parents as they grow old.)"

Zahir tried to counter the woman by saying how jihad was important to save the Muslims in Kashmir and stop Indian atrocities, but she would not listen to anything.

"Pecin aap samajh ke bhi na samjh ban rahe hain. Jab ki aap logon ke liye hum khun bahane ko raji hain, qurbani dete hain... aap jaison ki duua chahiye humhe. (Aunty you are pretending to not understand, when we are ready to sacrifice our lives for you people...we need your blessings.)" Zahir retorted.

The old woman laughed hysterically for a minute. Then she mentioned that if Zahir died for whatever cause he believed in, that would serve her no purpose. Her son died five years back. He had joined the jihad inspired by people like them, whom the old woman had given shelter. Aatish, the son, had been killed in an encounter.

"Shauhar toh pehle hi chal base the, aur ek lauta beta jo humhe Allah ne teen betiyon ke beech baksha unko aap log le gaye jihad ke naam. Par kya hasil huwa? Kya mere bete ka aapni jimmedari nibhana, budhi Maa ko dekhna, behnon ka nikaah karwana Jihad nahi tha? Apni zindagi ko sawarna bhi Jihad hain kyunki aap har mushkilon ke beech apno ka khayal rakhte hai... halaton ke saath jujhte hain...asli Jihad hai zindagi ke chunaution ke khilaf! (Husband had passed away earlier only. And the only son, whom god had gifted me after three daughters, was taken away by people like you in name of jihad. But what has been achieved? Was it not a jihad for my son to look after me in old age? Get his sisters married? Is it not a holy war to fight all difficulties and create a good life for oneself and others? To fight against the challenges of life is actual jihad.)"

Zahir was pained to hear this and it showed on his face. Karim looked at him and could gauge the level of compassion in his heart. Probably this path was not meant for Zahir. Neither was it meant for him.

Zahir wanted to hand over some cash to the old woman who refused by saying that if god has taken away one son from her, he has sent another one and that too with a band of boys.

Zahir looked questioningly at the lady, but she refused to reveal anything more and shut the door behind them.

Karim and Zahir had managed to reach Bandipora town after two days and two nights of an arduous trek. It was a small picturesque town located at a height of about 10,500 feet. Guarded by high cliffs on three sides and the Wular Lake on the south, the town sparkled in brilliant sunlight with its lush green fields and pristine water bodies.

Abbas Ghani ran a decent grocery store. He had agreed to lodge them for next few days on the condition that there would not be any trouble created by the duo. Abbas mentioned that the place had seen lesser militant activity compared to Kupwara, Sopore, Baramullah and Srinagar. Actually the contact who had been referred to Zahir for lodging with in Bandipora had left the town for some unforeseen circumstances. He had left a chit with his wife which instructed Zahir to approach Abbas for shelter. Abbas declared that people were peace loving and had started to lead a normal life. The terrain and the climate were the main reasons which kept the separatists at bay.

There were happy cheerful faces all around as the fugitives had started venturing into the marketplace, roads and lanes of the town. There was no pallor hanging in the air as could be felt in other places of Kashmir. Zahir commented, "*Yahan toh sab khushnuma hain, Karim Bhai.* Everyone looks so happy. There is neither fear nor mourning."

They had come across a bunch of school children comprising of both boys and girls headed to their school one cloudy morning. They were in the age group of ten to fifteen and frolicked like chirping birds as they walked. The boys wore white shirts and navy-blue trousers with checkered neck tie and the girls wore white salwars and blue kurtis. Some sported a Hijab while others did not. Karim and Zahir followed the group and reached the gate of their institution which bore the name 'Army Goodwill School, Bandipora'.

They witnessed many children inside the premises of the school, with both male and female teachers guiding them to their classes or indulging in various activities with them. Zahir could not hold back his surprise, "*Ladke aur ladkiyan ek saath padhai kar rahe hain? Hindustan Fauj ne school chalaya huwa hain yaha par toh aur humare taraf PoK me meri beheno ne thik se school dekha hi nahi. Pakistani Fauj ko kabhi aise nahi karte paya, pata nahi kya ho raha hain humhare saath.* (Girls and boys studying together and that also in a school run by the Indian Army! And in my village in PoK, my sisters have hardly attended school properly. The Pakistan army never supports us like this. Don't know what is happening with us.)"

Later in the day, while having lunch Abbas explained that Indian Army had started taking very good care of the people. They had opened schools, held free medical camps frequently where specialists came to advise people, and if needed, they were referred to the military hospitals in Srinagar or Udhampur. They also groomed youngsters to become respectable citizens.

"Arrey bhai, kahi bacchon ne Fauj join kiya, do ladke or do ladkiya Srinagar aur Delhi me medical padhai kar rahe hain, apna Bandipora Government school ke headmaster ka beta toh IAS officer ke liye chuna gaya hain. Ab din badal gaye Zahir bhai...halat waisa nahi raha. Logon ne khushhali aura aman ka rasta chuna hai (Brother, many kids have joined the army. Two boys and two girls are studying MBBS in Srinagar and Delhi, one son of our Badipora Government School headmaster has been selected and is undergoing training to become an IAS officer. Days have changed, Zahir bhai. Situation is not the same anymore. People are opting for happiness and peace.)"

Zahir looked absent minded. He then countered Abbas with the reports of army people harassing locals, beating them up, misbehaving with women and other atrocities. Abbas replied that he never heard soldiers misbehaving with any woman and as far as harassments were concerned, they happened as they had to often carry out search operations to nab militants hidden in the houses of people. He then gave a sly look towards Zahir and Karim and laughed.

Karim understood the latent dig. He was referring to them and it hurt Karim's self-esteem. They were militants absconding from security forces and this man had actually pointed that out indirectly.

"Par aap log befikr raho." Abbas assured them that they could stay safely in his house for a few more days, but it would be in their interest at this tender age to leave the path of militancy and resume normal lives.

Having narrated the story so far, Karim asked Zeenat to resume reading the diary from where she had left the previous day.

14

Zahir's Diary

Salma Aunty, Shazia and Aliah
19th August

In the last two months, I have not been able to write a single word. A lot happened since we had intruded into India. We had carried out our first attack on the Indian Army column on the Sopore-Kupwara highway. Then I and Karim had gone undercover in Bandipora for two weeks. But this was turning out to be a dangerous game, and mindless too. I don't know but a sense of futility is gradually seeping into me and the kind of support I was told I would get from the Kashmiris was not coming through.

Karim is a very good companion, who cares for me a lot, but he is not jihadi material. So far we had carried out three attacks in the Kupwara-Sopore belt, but he never could take an active part. His family had owned me as I had crossed over, so I feel very protective about him. In our last encounter we had lost five of our comrades, but there were no casualties on the enemy side. I doubt some locals had tipped off the army of our presence in the area. As things were getting murkier, I had let Karim go back to his village.

However, I had received a call from Shafiq Ahmed, a leader of the Jihad Council in Pakistan.

"Bhai Allah hafiz! Aap jis kaam ko Kashmir mai anjaam de rahe hain wo wakai tareef ke qaabil hai. Na sirf aapse sare Kashmiri, balki hamare Pakistani jihadi bhai bhi bohot khush hain. Aap ke gharwalon ko aap par beintehaa fakr hai, aakhir unka beta kitni bahaduri ke sath hindustani fauj ka mukabala kar raha hai. Zahir bhai, ek baat yaad rakhna, agar aapko kisi par mukhbiri ka shaq ho toh unko beshak maar dena. Jihad ke raaste me dhokhe aur maafi ki koi jagah nahi hai.

(The work you are doing in Kashmir is worth appreciation. Not only the Kashmiris, but the jihadis in Pakistan are very happy with you. Your folks at home are also very proud of the fact that you are bravely fighting with the Indians. But remember one thing, brother. If ever you are suspicious of somebody who is an agent of the Indian Army, just eliminate him. There is no scope for betrayal and pardon on the road to jihad."

He further informed that I have now been appointed as an Area Commander of Hijbul Mujahideen for the Kupwara district and the monthly remittance to my family in PoK has been doubled.

I do not know whether to be happy or sad. I miss my parents. I remember my mother a lot and whenever I meet an old woman tending to her sons, I well up with tears. Am I on the right track? My mother had asked me to follow the path of truth, but I remained confused in a maze of truth and deception. I had met several Kashmiris who despised me.

And there are so many houses which have lost a son or a brother in the name of this jihad. I must mention here about the old woman, Salma, whom we had met while travelling to Bandipora, after our first operation. While at Bandipora I had enquired about this lady and found the details that I am putting down here.

Salma has been living in this village since twenty-five years. Her husband had passed away at quite an early age and since then, she had raised her children, three daughters and a son, by running a small grocery shop that her late husband had set up. The grocery shop is located on the highway where the vehicles halt for a break and pick up sundry items for daily use, besides having a cup of tea or kahwa. The shop also catered to the villagers. Salma aunty barely managed to meet both ends from the income generated by the shop. Her only son Meraj used to help her run the shop since childhood. Gradually, by the age of eighteen, Meraj had started running the shop independently, while Salma managed the home and hearth with her three daughters.

One evening, a couple of strangers had come looking for Meraj and they had some discussions behind closed doors. When confronted by Salma, Meraj revealed that he had been in touch with some militants who had started frequenting the shop. He had sheltered them in the shop on a few occasions and had even hidden some weapons. Salma aunty was petrified. She and Shazia, the eldest of the children forbade Meraj to be associated with the militants and told him to immediately cease all contact with the outlaws. Meraj had agreed to abide by their wish and declared that he had asked the militants to stop connecting with him.

Few weeks passed peacefully. Shazia and Salma had started visiting the shop intermittently to ensure that Meraj remained away from the clutches of the jihadi group. Then one night the two terrorists had resurfaced and knocked on the door of the household. Meraj had denied them entry and requested them to leave. But they forced their way and demanded to stay in the house at gun point. The poor family did not have any other option but to accommodate them. They allowed only Shazia to go out of the house and run the shop and threatened to kill all of them if she divulged about their presence to anyone.

The poor woman and the siblings spent days and nights under tremendous duress and waited for the departure of the militants. The militants had promised to leave after a week when the hunt for them by the security forces would naturally die down. Salma, Shazia and the others abhorred each moment that they had to endure sharing the roof with these lumpens. They kept threatening the family, kept them under constant vigil and even made unwarranted advances towards the young girls.

Meraj was infuriated at this and warned the duo that if they ever tried to act funny, he would kill them, not caring for his life. Meraj was heavily built and stood at a height of six feet two inches. His appearance was intimidating and the terrorists had taken his warning seriously. However, soon the army had got a whiff of the terrorists and visited Shazia in the shop. Shazia had not revealed anything, but the army sleuths had followed her surreptitiously and could confirm the presence of the terrorists in the house. That same night, an army column had surrounded the village and came looking for the hidden militants to Salma aunty's doorsteps. The militants had asked Meraj to meet the troops outside the house and send them away by any means. No one knows what had transpired between the soldiers and Meraj, but the cordon was lifted up. Past midnight, seeing the troops leave, the terrorists had left the house, but insisted Meraj accompany them till the jungle behind the village. Meraj had no other alternative but to escort them. They had left the house and proceeded on the track at the backyard that led to the forests under the cover of the darkness. Salma and the daughters watched from the window as the three silhouettes merged away into the darkness of the night. Soon, the track was illuminated by search lights and they could see the three men momentarily freeze on their feet. In a fraction of a second there were sounds of firing and the two terrorists had dived to the ground. A confused Meraj had started running back to the house when to sheer horror of the women they noticed that one of the terrorists aimed his rifle towards Meraj and shot a burst of bullets. The poor lad let out a final trenchant shriek to collapse just few steps from the back door of the same humble dwelling where he had cried for the first time on this earth. But the two terrorists also did not live to relish their mindless violence. The jawans had pumped enough metal into their bodies.

There had been a furore over the killing of Meraj in the village as few politicians had tried to blame the army people for the killing of an innocent young man. They had tried to coax Salma aunty into giving a statement against the army. But she had stood her ground and refused to put the blame on the armed forces as she had seen the incident happening in front of her eyes.

I would never do such a thing in my life. It is cowardly to hide behind women and innocent people to save oneself from the enemy. I could not but silently appreciate the courage of the old lady and her conviction to stand by the truth. Also, the fact that there were such lecherous people in our ranks made me cringe with abomination. This is not the kind of jihad I have enrolled for.

The woman had lost her only son in this macabre fight for Jihad. She of course hated us but had given us some food for the night. She had mentioned that Allah had given her another son along with a troop. We did not understand. But while returning to Sopore from Bandipora, we again crossed by the old woman's house. Her house was decked up with decorative lights and a *shamiyana* (tent) was being erected adjacent to the dilapidated structure. As we closed in, to our horror we found several soldiers in uniform helping put everything into place. We kept observing from a distance. The old woman was in conversation with few other women, the bride standing in the midst of them. She was probably the woman's daughter. Then a tall man walked up to her, bowed down and touched her knees, a gesture of paying respect to elders practised by Indians as was informed by Karim in a hushed voice. She kissed the man, donning a Major's rank on the shoulder of his uniform, on the forehead. We could spot glistening streams rolling down her fair cheeks from that distance. The army man was leaving, but two young girls held him by his arms and refused to let him go.

I asked a passer-by what was going on. The man dressed up in a maroon sherwani, probably decked for an occasion, informed that the old woman's eldest daughter was getting married.

"Aap log idhar ke nahi lagte ho. Salma maasu ki beti Shazia ki shadi hain. Arrey bhai khush kismet ladki, Fauj ke Naik sahib ke saath nikah tay hua hain. Major Tripathy Sahab ko Salma maasu apna beta manti hain. Meraj, unka ek lauta beta khatm ho jaane ke baad se Tripathy sahab ne bahut khayal rakkha gharwalon ka. Unhone hi toh sab bandobast kiya hain. Ladka bhi unhone chuna hain. Wasim Lone, Kupwara se hain. Umdaa naujawan. Arrey barati aane ka waqt ho gaya.

(You people don't seem to be hailing from here. Salma aunty's daughter Shazia is getting married. Very fortunate girl, marrying a *Naik* from the army. Salma Aunty considers Major Tripathy as her son. Since Meraj, the only son of the old lady had passed away, Tripathy sir had looked after the family very well. He has only made all the arrangements including fixing the match. Wasim Lone, the groom, is from Kupwara. He is a very nice boy. Oh, it's time for the groom's party to arrive.

I did not know what to say. We call the likes of Tripathy infidels. But is this the way a kafir would look after a poor Muslim mother and her daughters?

Questioning my beliefs imposed by the Pakistani maulanas, I had moved away from the spot.

The only good thing that made me happy in the last few days in no uncertain terms was my acquaintance with Aliah.

As I lay in a room of a safe house in Sopore, her sweet voice still resonates around me. Her fragrance hangs in the air inside the room. She was here and we talked a lot. I spoke about my family back in PoK and she wanted to know everything in detail. She spoke about herself and her family who lived in a village near Baramullah. In fact, it was her voice that had struck me like a bolt from the blue when we had met for the first time in downtown Sopore. I was mesmerized by the lilt of her voice.

Few days back, I and Shahid, my accomplice from Pakistan, had carried a package of two pistols and ammunition to be delivered to a newly recruited man who had started acting as an informant for us. His house was located on the outskirts of the town. As we walked through the main street of Sopore, we observed that the army and police had established a checkpoint bang in the middle of the town. There was no bifurcation from there. They were checking each and every one. If we turned back and left, we would surely be spotted by the cops and apprehended or followed till our hideout. I quickly entered a furniture shop on one side of the road. After enquiring about prices of items like a casual customer, as I stepped out of the shop to see if the checking was being still carried out, I bumped into a girl. I was absent minded and the girl too was distracted, and it was she who had stumbled over my feet.

She apologized for her clumsiness and steadied herself. Then she pried into my eyes with a deep blue gaze accentuated by lines of kohl, through the thin opening of the *niqab* and asked if I was new in the town. As I stared at her, very much enthralled by the smoky inquisitive eyes, and the mellifluous voice, an idea had struck me suddenly. I asked her if she could keep the parcel (I did not mention it contained weapons) with her for some time as it contained holy manuscripts and I did not want them to be desecrated by the security guys at the check post. Women were not being frisked, so it would be safe with her. She asked me no questions and agreed readily. I handed over the parcel and told her that I would be collecting it from her after an hour, if she could wait for me in the fruit market, which was on the other side of town.

Looking back now, I know it was brash but also the only way to extricate ourselves from such a tricky situation.

We dilly-dallied for some time and then went through the checking point to the other side of the town. Shahid was skeptical about her turning up, but my hunch said otherwise. She had been there, waiting for us. Standing in front of a fruit shop and looking all around to spot us, I had felt a tinge of guilt in exploiting an innocent girl for our cause, but we had no other choice.

We gradually got acquainted. Aliah hailed from a poor family in the Baramullah area. She was studying in a coaching centre for competitive exams and stayed in a girls' hostel. She responded sympathetically when she heard about our true credentials as she said she had lost few of her relations in encounters with the security forces.

Aliah mentioned that it was not an easy thing for a thirteen-year-old girl to see her eldest sister banging her head on the dead body of her newly-wedded husband. Not even a month had passed after the marriage when her brother-in-law was caught in a gunfight between the militants and the police in their village. While the militants had fired upon the cops, she believed that the latter could have held fire. There were so many innocent men in the village, and as luck could have it, a stray bullet had caught her brother-in-law who had sneaked out of the house to put the motorcycle into the garage.

"I am not in favour of violence, Zahir. I blame both the

parties for my sister's misfortune, but see if you all can put an end to this menace. I will not participate actively, but can help you people out covertly as much as possible," she had said.

Shahid, who has also infiltrated along with me, turned out to be my closest aide. He is a little short-tempered and tends to act in a knee-jerk manner. We all have been radicalized on the path of jihad, but Sahid possesses a streak of unabashed brutality which I do not support. I have always believed that to execute jihad, we should inflict casualties on the security force personnel, but cold-blooded murder has never been my cup of tea. Probably because of this brazenness in Shahid, the Jihad Council in Balakote has warned me to keep him in check. His instantaneous reactions can often spoil a well-planned operation. Nevertheless Shahid is feared by all and in the unwritten hierarchy of our team, he is second to my position.

So, I had to be careful about Aliah and keep her guarded from the frantic assumptions of Shahid. Shahid kept telling me to be careful about her, but once I got her statements about herself verified from the coaching centre and our operatives in Baramulla area, he too began to be at ease with her. Our sources confirmed that Aliah Dar belonged to a poor family settled in the village of Narkote, who had left her home two years back to study in Sopore.

Today Aliah had come to take some money which was required to be sent to a Kashmiri youth's family in Sopore. This guy is fighting for us in the Baramullah area. We chatted for some time. She inquired why did the jihadi *tanzeem* (organization) in Pakistan did not look after the Kashmiri youth's families who were killed here fighting the cause of jihad.

She had many innocuous questions and seemed to be very compassionate about her people, their poverty, the mayhem and the economic state of Kashmir. I had no answers to most of her questions. But she was well connected with important people in the Kashmiri society, as claimed by her. She said that by virtue of her higher studies, she had many contacts in Srinagar and other towns of Kashmir. It had raised some questions in my mind, but I had brushed off the suspicions and wanted to enjoy her company.

I just basked in the solace of this new friend has brought in my life. As she speaks, I get absorbed in her deep blue eyes as placid as the waters of the Wular Lake and lose count of time. A small red mole sitting pretty on the ivory-white triangle of her swan-like slender throat, just below the cherry-shaped Adam's apple keeps distracting me and induces a mischievous urge of reaching out and feeling it with my hands. The beauty spot has a life of its own as it dances and changes colour with the sweet animated expressions of the beautiful girl. Her joys make it glow brighter and her sadness casts a somber shadow over it.

Aliah would raise her thin eyebrows seeing a smile breaking in on my bearded face and I would reply, "Nothing," reining in my virgin desires.

I am getting a bit tired and home-sick now. So much of bloodshed. Is it worth it? These Kashmiris can do without it. Thirty years have passed and there has been no solution. The people have started hating the mujahideen. At least the many I have come across in these towns and villages want to live peacefully. They have shut their doors on our faces. On many occasions, they have misbehaved with us. And the fear of guns or the lure of money is not working anymore. You can't buy out the souls of the people. And the scar here is soul deep.

I do not know how my parents are doing. I only got to hear about them from the members of the Jihad Council. Abbu and Ammi do not have mobile phones, so I have not spoken to them in the last six months. I had asked Musafir, an influential leader to make some arrangement so that at least I could hear their voices. The council have satellite phones with them and I could call through my mobile if they could send the phone to my house for a day.

I had also requested the council that if I could come back and meet my folks for a few days and return to Indian Kashmir. They had not agreed to that, saying it would be very risky to cross over repeatedly, and promised me that they would call me back after a certain period of time.

About the phone, Musafir had said he would do something, but he never got back to me. Do they really care for us? Anyway, I think Shahid has returned from the market. I have to cook now.

15

Zahir's Diary

Stone pelting

1st September

Today we have recruited ten more fresh youths into our cadre. Self, Shahid and Abid, a person in his thirties were the mastermind of the recruitment process. However, the procedure was narrated to us from across the border.

Shahid and Abid would roam around the market places, lanes and by-lanes of Sopore and its neighbourhood and pick out groups of youngsters. They would befriend them and try to know their pulse towards the Indian administration. I have seen this that the younger lots are easier to brainwash than the elderlies or the middle-aged people. The elderlies are contemptuous towards us and the middle-aged ones turn out to be scared of getting into trouble. The youngsters could be instigated and tempted by religious speeches, fear of bigotry if they did not support jihad and nominal amount of money in fomenting skirmishes with the Indian security forces.

And the easiest way of doing this is by pelting stones at passing army convoys or columns deployed on the ground.

A group of thirty energetic youths in the age group of fifteen to twenty were rounded up by Shahid and Abid. They had been divided into three groups and employed in collecting fragments of rocks from a nearby quarry. These were piled at places along the highway and in a hidden shed in one corner of the town.

Then one day, as a BSF (Border Security Force) convoy was approaching Sopore from Kupwara, these tyrants were let loose. They aimed at the vehicles and hurled stones at free will. Three of us, the mentors, took cover behind a grove and witnessed the havoc the stone pelters created. I was nervous that the security personnel would open fire, but Abid, who was more experienced than us assured that seeing the age profile of the boys, the forces would not fire at them. Glass shattered, blood flew in the air from the head of a couple of soldiers hit by stones, and vehicle bodies dented as the column barely managed to speed past the area avoiding further damage through the bedlam of the jubilation of the crowd and the chants of "Allah hu Akbar!" Not a single round was fired back at the miscreants. The crowd dispersed after this and we called the group leaders and handed them over the promised amount of money. We asked them to assemble the next day again in the town of Sopore and hurl stones at the army soldiers who established check points just in the middle of the town.

During the evening, these boys shifted the stones and placed them at different places on the sides of the main road that bifurcated the town. They were placed in such a manner that would not raise any suspicion and appear as if they were meant for some road repair work.

So the next day at around 10 a.m. our group assembled at designated places and started throwing bricks at the security personnel. The stones injured a few soldiers in spite of their helmets and shields. But the situation started going out of control. The shops downed their shutters and all the common people present in the market started running helter-skelter. Within a few minutes, there were a couple of stampedes and few civilians, old men and women, were badly injured. I was not prepared for this. I did not want the common people to be affected by this, but the frenzied youths had gone out of control. It was like mass hysteria. They did not even bother to look right and left and kept throwing the stones and inching closer to the barricades.

I spotted an old woman lying on the side of the road. She was trying to get up, but fell repeatedly as a couple of our boys stumbled over her while proceeding towards the barricades. I was appalled seeing that those buggers did not even stop to help her. I ran towards her and helped her stand on her feet. She had bruises on her face and trembled in shock and horror. I felt so pained seeing her condition, and her helplessness transported my mind back to my mother for a few moments. I dragged her and knocked on the door of a shop which had been closed down. A bearded man peeped out of the window beside the main door and seeing me, instantly tried shutting the window back on my face. But before he could do that, I caught hold of the guy by the collar of his kameej and pointed my pistol at him. I ordered him to open the door so that I could park the old woman there till the mayhem was over. He understood and allowed the lady inside. I backed off and retreated to hide behind the pillars of a billboard from where I had been witnessing the scene, satisfied that at least I was able to rescue one innocent pedestrian.

Soon, there was wailing of sirens and several armoured vehicles carrying more troops arrived at the spot. They disembarked quickly, took positions behind their vehicles and buildings and started firing tear gas shells. The whole area became filled with the caustic fumes that started causing our eyes to burn. The irritation in the eyes grew intense and through teary eyes I could see a couple of boys of our stone pelting group had been hit by something and had fallen down on the ground. The police and the army troops gradually started advancing through the smoky streets and nabbing few of our boys while the others fled. Abid mentioned that the boys who had been incapacitated had been hit by rubber pellets. They were not lethal, but if hit at vulnerable points in the body, could cause serious injuries.

Three of us met the leader of the boys in our secret hideout. We remunerated them and understood that the police had detained seven boys in the group. The leader extracted more money from us, claiming that he had to arrange lawyers for the arrested boys once they would be presented in the courts.

The saddest part was that the next day, we learnt from the local news that three ordinary people had been severely injured in the stampede and were hospitalized in critical conditions. Two of the boys who were pelting stones had eye injuries from the rubber pellets as well.

And what was the funniest part? A local political outfit which was driven by a pro-independence agenda called for a strike in Sopore the next day in protest of the atrocities by the police and armed forces in the city.

I was amused to realize that while the trouble was brewed by someone, executed by few others, and the mileage out of it was reaped by a third party. Politicians were the biggest manipulators anywhere in the world. But at the same time, introspectively, I abhorred the idea of this kind of cowardly fighting where innocents were harmed collaterally.

16

Zahir's Diary

Traitor among us
11th September

Today I feel like gunning down everybody associated with this so-called jihad. Abid, the calm, decent and most educated person in our group has been killed. Killed by deceit. This can't be real jihad.

Abid Dar belonged to a middle-class family from the town of Badgam, very close to the capital city of Srinagar. He had completed his engineering degree, but joined the jihadi group in Srinagar. He had participated in some activities and figured on a list of wanted terrorists maintained by the Srinagar police. The local Hijbul Mujahideen commanders of Srinagar had sent him to Sopore to work with us. He spoke very little, and had a pair of high-powered specs through which his intelligent eyes shone steadily. He would remain engrossed in books most of the day and tell me "*Zahir bhai, kitaben padha karo*...the more you read, the more you will know and have a broader vision."

Few days back, seven to eight of us were having a meeting on recruiting more youths from the Bandipora area when Abid was teased by Sameer, a local trader's son from Kupwara, who had joined hands with us. He had commented on how Abid had tried to become a *pundit* or a scholar. He wasted his time studying but at the end of it brushing butts with illiterates like the rest of us.

Abid, a serious man did not take to it kindly and had spoken his mind out. He retorted but patiently, pointing out fact after fact which many of us believed to be true. He addressed us all, commenting how at this age we were toting guns and killing people when our actual place should be in colleges and universities. This radicalism to save fellow Kashmiris by violence actually appealed to us because of the lack of education. Knowledge allowed people to think logically and distinguish between right and wrong. But we had all failed.

Sameer asked him, "Bhai, *par aap toh B-Tech kiye huye hain...phir aapne kyun hathiyar utha liya?* (Brother, but you have obtained a B-Tech degree, then why did you pick up arms?)"

Abid explained that many educated people like him were now repenting the day they had picked up arms. This mindless movement had been continuing for thirty years, but there was no end to it. Neither there would be.

"Kahi logon ki dukaane chalti hain isse...hum padhe hain toh samajh gaye par aap log nadan ho, nahi samjhoge aur maare jaoge. Par dukh is baat ki hain ki humhe is tarah phasaya gaya ki na idhar ke naa udhar ke...Jiyenge toh chhup ke jina padega... apne ghar nahi wapas jaa sakte hain kyun ki Hindustani fauj pakad legi aur aise chhup chhup ke ghut ghut ke ekdin khatam ho jayenge.

"Ghar me Abbu kidney ke patient hain, do bhai college aur school me padhte hain...do behne hain jinki shadi karani hain... aur main sab se bara chhup ke logon ko marta rehta hoon... hum sab ki yehi kahani hain."

(Many people run their business on this so-called Jihad. I am educated hence I can understand very well now. You people are innocent, hence can't see it yet. But alas, we are deeply stuck. We belong to neither this side nor that. We have to live in hiding. We can't go to our houses because the Indian security forces will nab us. We will keep suffering like this till we cease to exist one day.

My father is a kidney patient, two of my brothers are still studying in school and college; two sisters have to be married and I, being the eldest son, am killing people like a coward. We are all in the same boat.)

The eerie silence was broken by Shahid who lambasted Abid saying that it was Islam's fight and not about Kashmiri or Pakistani. Jihad is Allah's will to destroy the kafir. Abid asked Shahid if he had read the Quran properly, and if not, then not to speak unnecessary things about jihad.

"Aur Kashmir ke bare me kuch nahi jaante aap. He explained that the people we refer to as Kafir used to be the original inhabitants of Kashmir. Then about seven hundred years ago, Islam arrived and spread through teachings of Sufi saints to a great extent, and by force to some. In spite of that, here Muslims, Hindus and Buddhists used to cohabit peacefully. Some radical jihadis drove away the Hindus by committing atrocities on them. They poisoned the minds of the peace loving Kashmiris. Abid concluded without mincing any words about us Pakistanis by saying that these jihadis were fanatics

from Pakistan who had instigated the Kashmiris in the name of religion, creating mayhem.

I could sense Shahid getting infuriated. He growled at Abid and asked him to keep his views to himself only. This would have an ulterior effect on the youths who had joined us recently.

I dispersed the group. Shahid said that it would be best to eliminate Abid as he had diverted from the agenda. I did not like the idea. Abid was a good human being. I had seen him doing charity for the poor and the way he loved kids reflected the purity in his nature. I asked Sahid to leave him alone. But Shahid was cunning. He had got a whiff of my softness for Abid and proposed that Abid be made the commander of the raid planned on the small Central Reserve Police Force (CRPF) detachment, on the Bandipora road. This Central Police organisation looks after the internal law and order in Kashmir, mainly related to militancy and assists both the state police and the army in their operations. They are well equipped in terms of both, manpower and modern weapons.

This detachment used to be a break point for the convoys travelling on the road between Sopore and Bandipora. It was not heavily manned, and if attacked at night with a reasonable number of mujahideens armed with RPGs and rocket launchers, could be run over without facing much resistance.

I agreed, but failed to see the ploy behind this. The night the attack was planned, the detachment had a platoon (approximately forty troops) of CRPF halting for the night. The security was beefed up. I suspect now that Shahid knew about this and had chosen that night purposefully. The attack was repelled. Seven out of the ten of our cadres were killed in the operation. Abid was one of them. But my sources say he had managed to disengage himself from the spot and was gunned down by one of our team members. It was a cold-blooded murder of an unsuspecting member of our team by an insider.

Who else could it be, other than...

17

Zahir's change of mind

"So who was it that Zahir suspected killed Abid? Did he tell you?" Zeenat closed the diary and asked Karim.

Karim looked out of the window, seemingly lost in thought for some time and then replied that though Zahir had never mentioned it clearly, but Karim felt that he hinted at Shahid. The fact was that at this point Zahir had started growing uncertain and suspicious about the people around him. Zahir had mentioned to Karim, when later they had met before the former's exfiltration, that it was a very dirty game. No one knew who was being used and exploited by whom. Karim pointed at the diary and said that the same had been written there in his account.

"And what happened to Aliah? Did he not even trust that girl?" Zeenat demanded to know.

"Well, it's all about her in the next few pages of the diary. You can read for yourself," Karim's words carried a request inherently for him to be left alone. Long sessions had taken place for the last two days and it was taxing upon a man who was still healing from surgery.

Col Manav took the cue and directed Zeenat to pause the interactions for the day.

"You rest buddy. We shall return after a couple of days. Have to take care of something in between. In the meantime, you go through this form and fill it up as much as possible. We shall guide you to complete it wherever you get stuck." Col Manav handed over a piece of paper that contained the details of instrument of surrender of a terrorist to the authorities.

Zeenat, who was holding the diary requested Karim if she could carry it along with her so that she could finish reading it in the next two days. Karim agreed but said that he intended to post it back to the writer someday as he knew how important it was for the person.

Zeenat promised to return it safely to him and assured him that it was equally important to her.

Karim looked at her quizzically and could find no answer in her serene smile that travelled from the curvy lips along the rosy cheeks to settle softly on the corners of the azure eyes.

Karim looked away but did not hesitate to marvel at the exquisite beauty of the young Army Captain.

Karim's mother requested the duo to have lunch, which they politely refused.

"*Mere bete ko bacha lena aap log. ...masoom hain behek gaya tha.* (Save my son...He is innocent, had got forced into this.)" the lady held Zeenat by her arm and welled up.

Both the officers assured her of the best of their efforts to help Karim and left the house.

18

Sisterhood in uniform

Zeenat returned to her quarter inside the cantonment and kept the diary on her study table. She would read it later in the night. After a quick shower and lunch, she waited for the arrival of Poonam and her parents who wished to visit Kashmir.

Poonam Sharma was her batch-mate from the training days in OTA in Chennai. She had been posted to Pathankot since her commissioning and had expressed her desire to visit Kashmir with her parents.

Zeenat had been delighted as Poonam was not only a mere batch-mate, but the best buddy she had made outside Kashmir. She fondly remembered their cadet days in OTA.

While Zeenat had been physically very fit and stubborn about winning over challenges, Poonam had been finding it difficult to cope with the rigorous training standards. Zeenat had understood that selection in the armed forces was not merely dependent on physical fitness. The service selection board interview process was in fact one of the most difficult interview sessions of all competitive exams in India and encompassed physical fitness, personality assessment, intelligence quotient, dynamics of group behaviour, leadership traits and psychological assessment. One could be very intelligent to qualify for IIT or could be an excellent sportsman to become an international level athlete, but unless he or she could match the parameters the army was looking for to endure the challenging yet stressful career, the selection was virtually impossible.

Poonam and Zeenat had got along from the very first day in the training academy. They shared the same cabin and developed a bond of mutual trust and respect. Zeenat had found Poonam to be the most empathetic person amongst all her batch-mates. She was full of sympathy when she came to know about Zeenat's background and acted as a bridge with other trainees for all the cultural differences that existed between Zeenat and the other cadets from different parts of the country. Not many girls from Kashmir had joined the Indian Army prior to Zeenat.

Zeenat, on the other hand, assisted Poonam in clearing all her physical tests. When the other cadets used to rest after their hectic training schedules, Zeenat would drag Poonam to the physical training grounds and make her practice chin ups, horizontal rope climbing, vertical climbing and toe-touches. They used to run together circling the PT fields so that Poonam could pass her 2.4 km and 5 km runs.

They sweated in the training together. The day used to start at four in the morning. Some days, they would slip into their olive-green uniforms, rush to collect the rifles from the kote and be present in the drill square to undergo a grueling session of a drill followed by immediate changing to PT gears of t-shirts and shorts and attend the PT classes. On other days, the morning schedules were same, only the events were reversed. After a quick break for showers and breakfast, they would then rush to the academic classes or attend weapon training in squad posts. These would be interspersed by periodic live firing sessions, swimming and diving classes, obstacle courses and games. All these activities in the scorching heat of Chennai were no mean tasks to achieve. From polishing shoes to shining the metals in the uniforms with brasso, getting the cabins inspected by officer instructors to learning the correct manner of having meals at the dining tables with forks, spoons and knives in the antique Officers' Mess, the youngsters were being groomed to become excellent leaders. Leaders who would be revered and respected by the populace, irrespective of caste, creed and religion.

The cadets were tested by the instructors periodically and they had to pass the tests theoretically, physically and practically in order to earn the stars on their shoulders. They also had to undergo two camps outside the premises of the academy to apply their learnings on simulated real-life situations. The training would culminate with the most arduous and significant tactical exercise that formed a part of the second camp. A night navigational route march for about fifty kms with full battle loads.

Once the cadets completed this route march, the body and mind would have been stretched till the limits of endurance. Zeenat excelled in most of the trainings and was running for the best female cadet in her course, brushing shoulders with another cadet, Amita Nayak. Poonam, assisted by Zeenat, had also successfully completed the training.

Zeenat received Poonam and her parents in the late afternoon that day in the Kupwara cantonment. The two friends hugged like long-lost sisters. They had remained in touch, but had not been able to meet up after their commissioning almost three years ago. They had lots to catch up on. Zeenat had arranged for a guest room for Poonam's parents and insisted that Poonam stay with her in her apartment. The Sharmas had visited Srinagar, Gulmarg and Sonmarg before coming to the Kupwara district and Zeenat had applied for two days of leave to show them around the places of interest.

They all dined together and reminisced about the good old training days. A story that would always feature while talking about training was how Poonam was dragged out of the swimming pool in the OTA after a dive.

It was during the first half of the training when the girls had to pass a test of twenty-five metres of swimming and take a dive from a twenty-foot board into the swimming pool. Both Zeenat and Poonam had been dead sinkers with no experience in swimming, but Zeenat was a fast learner. She had managed to learn to cover the distance by staying afloat after jumping into the pool then paddling some distance ahead, before fiercely swinging her arms to reach the other side. She was gradually learning the technique of free style swimming and was confident of becoming a reasonably good swimmer with another couple of months of practice.

But Poonam had not been that adept then. She was still finding it difficult to move ahead in the water. On the day of the incident, both the cadets were lined up on the diving board to take a jump. Poonam had a fear of heights, which she was trying her best to overcome. It could be a bit overwhelming for many standing at that height, looking down at the water, while the entire Chennai's horizon stared back at you. The instructors always asked the cadets to look straight and drop straight into the water. Once the the gravity pulled the divers to the basement of the pool, the cadets were required to push on the floor of the pool with their legs, gain the buoyancy and strike the water downwards with both arms to rise gradually above the surface of the water. If one looked down, the sight could be enervating with everyone and everything looking smaller than their usual dimensions and the blue surface of the pool rippling and splashing, inviting them with its underlying mysteries.

Poonam was hesitating to take the plunge, in spite of the shouts of the instructors and pepping by the other cadets. On insistence of one of the instructors, Zeenat had suddenly pushed Poonam into the pool. She had fallen like a dead log and sunk under the water. Generally, an individual would come up within ten to fifteen seconds, and then the next cadet on the diving board would jump. But when after twenty odd seconds, Poonam had not emerged on the surface, Zeenat felt pangs of alarm for her friend. Though she had not till then acquired the skills fully, without any further thought, she had dived head down into the water, something only expert swimmers could do. As she had hit the water with head first, from the corner of her eyes she had caught the swimming *ustaad* also diving from the side of the pool to rescue Poonam.

Zeenat had reached the bottom of the pool and found a shocked Poonam frantically trying to climb up, but her efforts and technique were not good enough to give her the buoyant lift. She was not taking the leap with the support of her legs. Zeenat had managed to take a curve and straighten herself from the foetal posture owing to her tremendous agility that even the pressure of the water could not weigh down. At the same time, the swimming ustaad Deviah Sahab had also reached the spot. Both of them had delicately held Poonam by her armpits on either side and resurfaced to the relief of all present in the pool. Poonam had gained her courage and composure seeing her friend and the ustaad, and had remained calm contrary to the panic that sinking people resorted to under the water.

Zeenat was highly applauded for her bravery and since then, the bonding between the two girls increased manifolds.

Also, when the best cadet was to be selected on completion of the training, that feat of Zeenat had helped her to surge past Amita Nayak in winning the distinction.

Three years had passed since then, and the friends had moved to respective postings. They caught up like old times and there was much to be told and heard. Poonam's parents casually brought up the topic of marriage, to which both the friends had giggled and expressed their reluctance. They wanted to live the adventures the Army was providing them for a while longer, unhindered and unbridled.

After settling the parents in the guest room, Zeenat and Poonam retired for the night in Zeenat's apartment. They gossiped for some time before a weary Poonam dozed off.

Zeenat then switched on the bedside lamp and opened Zahir's diary. She was intrigued by it.

As she kept flipping through the pages, the faint light of the lamp played on with the changing emotions showing on her face; from the furrowed eyebrows to the creases on the forehead and from the curves of the lips to the shadows in the eyes.

19

Operation Iris

Col Manav was sitting in his office inside the Kupwara cantonment going through the reports of the intelligence operatives spread across the district. The top secret reports elaborated upon the clandestine activities of terrorists, mujahids, sympathizers and over ground entities that secretly helped militancy in the garb of a clean image in the society. All these people and agencies had to be either eliminated or reformed. The local Kashmiris had done away with the initial frenzy of separation from India painted rosily by the jihadis from across the border. They had seen enough blood and gore to understand that they were just being used as a pawn by a nation that could not look after its own citizens properly. The wretched condition of population in Sindh and Baluchistan had to a great extent blown the cover from the face of Pakistan as a saviour of Islamic population in the region and bared the ugly hypocrisy.

Col Manav had understood one thing in his career spanning over twenty-five years in the Army. Battles were won in the mind. While the arsenal may determine a military weight, in the domain of sub conventional warfare, the elements of surprise, deception and covert, all constituting psychological factors are the most important deliverables up a warrior's sleeve.

Since last three decades, Pakistan sponsored mujahideen have been trying to alter the psyche of Kashmiris towards a pro liberalisation or pro Paki stance. Countless bullets and explosives by kilos had been used to prevent this nefarious design. But a point had arrived when it was realised that to win this proxy war, besides the brawn, the brain had to be used amply. The Indian military came up with many welfare measures aimed at winning the hearts and minds of the people in the valley, WHAM actions as they were called fondly and formed the basis of an operation called Op Sadbhavna.

Along with this, the military intelligence started devising newer methods and operated by countering the radical imposition on the masses in Kashmir. And Col Manav was passionate about this, his domain of expertise.

In general, Kashmiris realized that it was in their best interest to remain a part of India, rather than be independent. As more and more people became educated, the Kashmiris realized that their land was always an integral part of India, since ancient times. If they ceded from India, their condition would not be any better than Pakistan, which had disintegrated, inspired by the personal ambition of few politico-religious evangelists. In the eventuality of being independent, it would be only a matter of time before Pakistan seized the territory under its flag. Then it would be an unending struggle to liberate from the clutches of a nation that had horrendous records of human rights.

The phone rang and the exchange operator informed that the Corps Commander wanted to have a word with Col Manav. Manav used to report to the Divisional commander, but on a particular project, he rendered his reports directly to the GoC of the Corps.

"Manav, how are you doing? Boxy this side."

Lt Gen Tarun Bakshi, the Corps commander was referred to by this unusual name since his youngster days. There were two cadets with the surname Bakshi in one particular batch in Indian Military Academy. Tarun Bakshi had been a services boxer during the training and few initial years of service. Fondly, he was addressed as "Bakshi the boxer" by his course mates to distinguish him from the other Bakshi. Since then, the name had got altered a bit to "Boxy" and the General had started taking a liking to the address.

"I hope the project Iris is on track? What is the latest on this?" The GOC demanded after the two had exchanged the customary greetings.

"Yes sir, the area of intended ops has been marked. Targets identified and the script prepared. The agent has been given a free hand to go about this with all support from a designated team. We have also been able to successfully infiltrate the militant groups in the area. Important info on their moves and plans are rolling in bits and pieces," Manav replied confidently.

"Good. But Manav, we do not want this to be a free for all. I hope the targets are selected based on their merits and importance? Also, focus in the pockets where the discontent still prevails. Segregate these targets and proceed with the op dynamics. Rest of the hardliners can be handled by our battalions operating on ground."

"Yes sir, we are proceeding as per the roadmap drawn and discussed in your office the other day." Manav assured the General.

"I am sure your agent will do a fantastic job, being well-trained and much matured. So your first target has crossed over the fence? Zahir, the area commander, I guess?" The GOC inquired.

"Zahir has left sir. We are tracking his accomplice, Shahid. This guy is a mindless fanatic sir. With Zahir gone, he is trying to take over as area commander. We have to nab him soon. He has been spotted in a tourist lodge in Sonmarg. The handler Masood has been arrested."

"Very well. Keep it clean Manav. No unnecessary bloodshed. All the best. Keep me informed. Jai Hind!" The call was disconnected.

Manav reclined on his chair and looked at the map of Kashmir hanging on the wall across him with a faint smile on his lips. Op Iris was on a roll.

20
Nabbing Shahid

After back-to-back attacks on the CRPF camp and a BSF convoy, the situation in the Sopore area had worsened. The noose of vigilance had become excruciatingly tight with the security forces and the police carrying out intense search operations to nab the culprits. There were several new check-posts established at various places. Both Zahir and Shahid had decided earlier to leave the area and go underground immediately after the CRPF camp attack. While Zahir had decided to head towards Bandipora, Shahid had intimated that he would park himself in the state capital Srinagar. They had moved out early in the morning, following the night of the attack without much exchange of words. Shahid had rejoiced within himself, noticing the crust of firm grimness that had descended upon the face of Zahir before leaving. He was happy for himself and knew what was in store for both of them. He had tipped the local boy Jehangir handsomely and asked him to look after Zahir properly as the latter was an asset for their movement.

Shahid had however not moved to Srinagar immediately. Instead, he had continued staying in a small village few kilometres away from the Sopore town and decided to keep a watch on the situation. However, when the patrols of the army started frequenting areas very close to the remote village, he decided to move out. The vigour in the combing operations did not seem to reduce in the Kupwara district. In fact, quite a few local youths who had participated in stone pelting had been rounded up and sentenced to a small period of imprisonment.

One morning, after lying underground for almost a month, Shahid left Sopore with Bilawal, an infiltrator like him, and Nawab Gilani, a local youth. Shahid had initially planned to bring only Bilawal along with him, but at the last moment, he had remembered something. There was this young man Nawab who used to talk a lot about his life as a horse handler in a village near the popular tourist place of Sonmarg. He would often mention he had good contacts with many tour operators in the area and urged both Zahir and Shahid to visit the place, as it was one of the most beautiful places in Kashmir. Neither Zahir nor Shahid had any intention of going for sightseeing, but the idea of a place thronged by tourists had struck Shahid's mind as a probable hiding place.

Shahid had informed a common contact the night prior to the day of his move about ensuring that Nawab accompanied him. Nawab stayed in his uncle's house in the Sopore town. The boy was almost dragged out of his slumber and asked to accompany Shahid and Bilawal. He was told that they would be going to Srinagar and required his assistance in running errands while they would remain confined to their hideout.

Bilawal was dressed as a woman and wore a burqa over his phiran. He was short in height for a man; standing at 5 feet 5 inches. Clean shaven, his anatomy was modified with enhancers to make him look like a veiled woman. This was primarily done for hiding two pistols in the ladies' vanity bag and fragmented parts of two rifles in a bag meant for the lady. There would be hardly any lady cops on the highway check points and the male cops or the security forces personnel never frisked women or their luggage.

When the cab had travelled for about an hour, the party had encountered a military check post. The soldiers checked the vehicle and the credentials of the persons travelling. When one young soldier pointed at the pink-coloured duffle bag kept in between Shahid and Bilawal sitting on the rear seat, the latter mimicked the voice of a woman and defiantly said, "*Auroton ke kapde dekhne ka itna shauk hai bhaiya aapko?* Why so curious about women's clothes?"

The soldier was embarrassed and tried to justify when Shahid joined in the protest. "*Aap log aise kisi aurat ko beizzat nahi kar sakte hain. Yeh humhari auroton ki aabru ka sawal hain...* (You people can't insult women like this...this is the question of honour of our women.)"

The soldier stepped back and Shahid patted the driver on his back to move when a *Havildar,* probably the commander of the check post stepped in. He had probably not liked the tone in which both Shahid and Bilawal had spoken. He asked them to stop and park the vehicle to a side of the road and informed them that he would call for female police personnel from the nearest police station. They would have to wait till the bag was searched.

Shahid understood that he had worsened a pretty normal situation to a complex one by being unnecessarily rude. He had stepped out of the cab and pleaded with the Havildar in a mellowed down manner. But the senior soldier would not budge. At this point of time, Shahid found an uncanny saviour in Nawab who had all that long been out of sight and mind. He stepped in and led the Havildar away to talk in privacy. After five minutes, he returned and asked the driver to move. The young soldier and the Havildar looked at them through squinted eyes as the cab sped past the check point.

A jubilant Shahid playfully slapped on the back of the head of Nawab and asked him what he had done to manage the safe extrication. Nawab smiled without turning his head back to them and said that he had few relatives in the administration and a reference worked.

After this, they had kept moving and reached Sonmarg around noon. They checked into a tourist lodge recommended by Nawab, situated on the outskirts of the small town. Sonmarg, situated at an altitude of about nine thousand feet and surrounded by lofty snowy peaks and pristine blue lakes offered a good hide-out potential. The place was thronged by the more adventurous of the tourists at that time of the year, when winter had started to creep in, spraying the earth and the vegetation with the season's fresh layers of snow. Tourists mainly visited the place to gain a first-hand experience of the snowfall and also to trek till the Thajiwas glacier that stood like an enormous cone of flashing ivory to the south of the town. During the early monsoon months, the Hindu pilgrims assembled at Sonmarg and were escorted by the local guides to the holy Amarnath shrine situated in the midst of the lofty snow-clad peaks of the ancient Himalayas.

As Shahid and Bilawal checked into the tavern as Mr and Mrs Shahid Yunus, Nawab excused himself and said he would stay at his home in a nearby village. His father and two brothers used to own ponies which were hired by the tourists for sightseeing. In leaner phases like winters, they grazed sheep and ran a small pharmacy shop in the town. Shahid informed the manager of the lodge that they had come for match making for his brother with a sister of Nawab and would stay put for a few days. They would also do some sightseeing. He also requested that they should not be disturbed unnecessarily, as his wife who was a very orthodox and pious woman, was slightly under the weather. She needed to rest.

Having convinced the manager, the duo settled in their room on the first floor of the double storey dwelling. They had rented the corner-most room out of the seven in a line. The windows of the room opened to a balcony which faced a cluster of oak trees peering over the track that led to the glacier. The chilly winds kissed colder by the glacier ruffled leaves of the trees before untiringly strumming on the window panes.

Bilawal was dying to shed off the burqa and the other embellishments of womanly appearance. He returned to his own avatar as soon as they had checked inside the room. Shahid warned him to keep the curtains of the windows drawn and not to venture there without wearing a burqa. They bathed, called for lunch inside the room and ensured that Bilawal was in the bathroom whenever the waiter would come to deliver something. Shahid was carrying a lot of money and he tipped the waiter handsomely. He did not want too many people coming to the room and hence after few minutes of polite familiarization insisted that the same waiter serve them whenever they would require something.

Bilawal brought out the rifle parts and assembled them to full weapons. It was better to remain prepared for any contingency. The rifles were then hidden behind clothes inside a cupboard mounted on the wall.

Shahid took their washed clothes and hanged them on a wire meant for putting clothes for drying in the small attached verandah facing the grove of the oaks. What he failed to notice was that a frail man in Kashmiri attire, obscured behind a giant oak tree, was looking towards the verandah through a pair of binoculars.

The day and the night passed off peacefully. Shahid was happy to have changed the plans at the last moment and come to this non-descript place to remain under cover for some days.

The next day, as Bilawal was getting impatient and feeling claustrophobic inside the room, Shahid decided to go out for some time and take a stroll in the small picturesque town. Bilawal got into her female avatar and the couple walked till the road that led to the glacier. Few tourists were walking and riding on ponies towards the meadow, littered with stones of various sizes and criss-crossed by streams, that lay stretched at the foot of the Thajiwas glacier. There were local Kashmiris lined up along the route selling *shilajit,* a sticky sedimentary substance formed on the Himalayan rocks by the decomposition of plants on mineralized surface, and *kasturi* oil derived from the navel pod of a species of musk deer family available in the higher reaches of the mountains, famous for its unique musk fragrance. Shahid cursed at the local Kashmiris who gleefully mingled and pleaded with the tourists, most of whom he perceived were kafirs. Disgusted, they walked back to the hotel and ordered for lunch in the room.

In the evening, the receptionist informed that Nawab had come to meet them and waited in the lobby. Shahid had instructed the hotel staff to avoid sending any visitor to the room. He went down to meet Nawab and instructed Bilawal to remain dressed as a woman, which the latter complained about, as it was tiring putting the dress on and off several times in the day.

In the lobby, Nawab was sitting with a middle-aged man in his mid thirties. He introduced the man as Abu Malik, an elderly cousin of his. Nawab had brought some gosht cooked at home for them and they talked sitting over cups of tea. Abu seemed to be a jovial man and spoke about how the Kashmiri people were toiling hard to earn money from tourism, which had started to gain momentum after many years. He enquired about Shahid's wife and hoped she was keeping well. Shahid switched past the topic hastily and then the man asked something that foxed him.

"*Aap ki biwi kya ladkon ki nikkar pehanti hain?* (Does your wife wear man's underpants?)"

Shahid immediately realised the blunder he had made the previous afternoon. Still, he tried to remain unfazed and demanded coldly what kind of nonsense the man was speaking? He was about to stand up and head for his room when Abu instructed him to keep sitting.

"Janab aap do do ladkon ke nikkar aur buniyan sukhne dale the balcony me... ladkon ke kapde dikhe par koi madam ke libaas dhulai nahi huyi kya! (Sir, you had put out two sets of underpants and vests for drying in the balcony. Men's clothes could be seen hanging, but does the lady not wash her clothes?)"

As Shahid fumbled for an answer, he observed the black barrel of a Beretta M9 pistol peeping out of the shawl wrapped around Abu's solid frame. It was aimed at his stomach. He instructed Shahid to call up his room and inform his wife that Nawab would be coming to deliver the tiffin carrier to the room. Shahid had carelessly left his pistol in his room as he had not expected Nawab to be a threat. He did as instructed. Nawab smiled at him and like a leopard sprang up the stairs with the food container. Few minutes later, Bilawal in a cardigan and pyjamas was seen climbing down the stairs, prodded by an ecstatic Nawab from behind. In a matter of minutes, the operation to nab Shahid and his accomplice was over without a single shot being fired.

A team of local police and soldiers was waiting outside.

"Shahid Kaksar, ISI *ki training aur yeh laprwahi?*" Abu, alias Major Anwar, and Nawab, an accomplice of the Army Intelligence handed over the guys to the police and merged away into the shadows of the starry evening that had descended over the ridges and the valley.

21

Zahir's story continues

After spending a couple of days' well-deserved break and enjoying the leisure time with Poonam and her parents, Zeenat rejoined her duties. She met Col Manav and briefed him about the remaining contents of the diary. She became exhilaratingly happy when she came to know about the apprehension of Shahid and Bilawal, because Nawab was someone whom she had hand-picked to be a part of the Army's intelligence team. Zeenat narrated the final events in life of Zahir's life before he had exfiltrated almost a month back.

Zahir's Diary

Narrow escape and the injury

24th December

Srinagar, the capital city of Kashmir. I saw the Dal Lake for the first time today. I have heard so many things about this beautiful water body since my childhood, but never thought that one day my life would bring me to it and make me realise that the visual treat actually far exceeded the superlatives used about it.

When I had stood by the lake in the morning, I could find colourful *shikaras* lined up on the shore, separated by jetties which were still covered by the thick layers of snow from the previous night's fall. A group of soldiers patrolling the area walked past me. But I do not cringe at their sight now. They waved at me as I smiled at them.

The winter sun softly melted away the mist which had cascaded down from the heavens since dawn, pushing the valley into a stupor of white languor. The rays of the sun spreading everywhere, woke the town up as gradually the frosty roof tops, streets and the trees bathed in the golden warmth. From the din and bustle around me, who would say that there is an undercurrent of insurgency in this area.

Life seemed to go on as usual, unless people like us threatened to cause disruptions. A group of tourists bargained with a house boat owner as another giggling group engaged in photography.

The surface of the lake gradually became visible as the chinks in the icy armour plate cover widened to give way to the underlying chilly waters emitting cold steam. The slabs would melt through the day and lay bare the vast expanse of the turquoise blue waters for the eyes to behold till wherever they could reach.

I consider myself lucky that today my eyes can travel far and wide. I can behold the beautiful creation of God around me. But it could have been entirely different. So l must write down what happened in the past two months since Abid had been killed in an operation against the CRPF.

Safely enjoying the hospitality of the Dar house situated in a quaint corner of the city, I have decided to return tomorrow.

The doctor had said that my eyes have healed reasonably and I have to just keep applying the medicines. I shall go to Karim's village and then retreat the way I had entered. It's been almost a year since I have been away from home. I have not informed anyone about the decision, neither here nor in PoK as I do not trust anybody except Aliah and Karim. I have already sounded Karim to make an arrangement with the handler Masood, who had sneaked us in to help me egress. But I do not know how and what to tell Aliah. She has been hell bent on accompanying me to PoK, marry and settle down there. I shall have to convince her that I shall get her over there once I safely reach myself.

I have fallen in love with her madly. For someone like me, who hailed from a very primitive and ultra-conservative society in PoK, where even today, free interactions between boys and girls are considered as taboo, getting attracted to a beautiful and independent girl like Aliah was quite natural. The untended spring of youth had suddenly awakened to the soft cores of femininity that Aliah had brought in like fresh air carried on her whiffs of lavender perfumes, starkly pleasant in the midst of the pungency of metals and explosives.

She had several times over the past few months asked me to either surrender or go back to PoK. And eventually, I had become convinced. To this environment of mirth and tact I did not belong anymore. I had become disillusioned. But I did not let others know about my state of mind. I kept in touch with the council in Pakistan and let Shahid plan and execute the acts of terrorism. This made him feel important, as he got a chance to emerge from my shadow and had started behaving like the area commander already.

Now let me go back to the time after Abid's assassination.

After a few sporadic actions, I had moved to a hideout in a village situated on the axis towards Bandipora. I had a local boy from Bandipora, Jehangir, who would be my buddy during this period of hibernation. We never stayed alone and always operated at least in a pair. It was a small village of about twenty houses in the higher altitudes of the mountains. I was cut off from all communication and only Shahid knew about my location, as he would need to reach out to me in case of any requirement.

One early morning, when dawn was about to break, I was woken up by dogs barking loudly. My instincts and experiences hinted at something unusual. As I put on my shoes and was about to step out, the owner of the house came knocking on the doors of our dingy room. He informed that the village had been cordoned off by the army and the *sarpanch* had asked him to hand over the two of us to the Army. The *sarpanch* soon entered the house and started pleading with us to surrender, otherwise there would be firing inside the village. I refused to surrender because all I wanted then was to go back home. I did not want to pursue with this dubious cause, neither did I want to get stuck here. I told this to both the village elders in no uncertain terms. The owner of the house understood, but the headman kept nagging. Finally he gave up and asked me to leave surreptitiously, without causing any trouble for the villagers.

Army cordons are generally placed all around a settlement. And a team then enters the village going from house to house in search of hidden militants. I had to be quick and leave before the soldiers started the search operations. The house owner mentioned that there was a dry bed of a stream that flowed at the western fringe of the village. A drainage trench from the village was well connected to the stream for carrying excess water. And there was a culvert at the junction of the drain and the stream. He asked us to use the drain to crawl to the culvert and then escape through the path of the water channel downstream. The waterfall was dry at that point of the year and had excellent cover of bamboo groves at many places. I had carried out a general recce of the area earlier. We could hit the road to Bandipora or even reach other remote villages through mountain tracks.

As we picked up our rifles and other stuff in small kit bags, the announcement for us to surrender blared through the village air. We ducked into the drainage trench and scuttled for a few minutes before reaching the culvert. We were under the culvert catching up our breath, resting against boulders when the area above our head became illuminated. There were whispers. Soldiers talked with each other. They had probably sensed our movement. Before I could gesture at Jehangir to keep calm and still, the seventeen-year old lost his nerves. He fired, aiming at the voices and then all hell broke loose. There was heavy fire of automatics from the upstream direction. Initially the soldiers could not guess our location. Jehangir started crawling back towards the well. He was gone beyond the point of damage control. I had to look after myself. I just dived on the dry water bed of the stream and rolled down. There was a bright flash followed by a loud bang and then I felt something very sharp hit me on my face just below the right eye. It was a grenade lobbed probably under the culvert to flush us out. The impact was so forceful that I was thrown away several yards down the stream. My rifle flew away from me and landed into a bamboo grove. The darkness of the night grew several shades blacker as I managed to steady myself and sat on my haunches for a few seconds. My head reeled and heart throbbed in response to the extreme action. Once I was sure there were no bullets being fired at me, I sneaked into a shrubbery and slipped into the deeper jungles beside the ravine.

My vision had become blurred and I barely managed to see clearly. As the commotion from the village and the sound of fire shots became fainter, I heard the cackling of water nearby and spotted another rivulet flowing down a narrow gorge. I stepped into the water and splashed a few handfuls onto my eyes. The reddish water trickled down my cheek and drenched my phiran. After several rounds of splashing and pressing with the handkerchief, the bleeding stopped. My vision became a bit clear, but I was having double sight of everything around. The eyes had been affected. I managed to continue my journey further away from the village under cordon and aligned myself towards the highway. I knew what to do.

After loitering for an hour or so, I came across a settlement on a ledge of the mountains just above the highway to Bandipora. It was a sprawling colony of modest looking houses which spoke of the level of affluence of the people. I spotted a house with a signboard flashing a doctor's name and a red cross inscribed beside it. The dawn was breaking as I knocked on the door. The doctor himself opened the door and was scared seeing a man with a bloodied face standing in front of him at such an unearthly hour. I shoved him inside and closed the door after entering the house.

I had no choice but to divulge everything. The man started creating a ruckus, asking me to leave. He was afraid that soon the army or police would come calling after me and his peaceful abode would be turned into a battlefield. I pleaded with him that I required first aid, and as soon as he would dress me up, I would leave. There were sleepy eyes peeping from behind the curtains hanging on a door that probably led to the inner quarters from the room where we were talking.

When the doctor did not budge in spite of cajoling earnestly, I took out the pistol and kept it on the table in front of him. At this point, a fat woman in a house coat came shrieking from inside and started crying hysterically. I once again assured both the husband and the wife that the earlier the doctor tended to my wounds, I would leave. The point sunk in.

The doctor examined my eyes and removed minute debris of wood and shards of metal from the flesh below my eyes. He then dressed up the area and said I needed to see an ophthalmologist as soon as possible, because there could be greater damage to my eyes.

I spotted a telephone in one corner of the room and used it to call Aliah. She was alarmed hearing my plight and said that she would be reaching me as soon as possible. I gave her the address. Then, to much of anguish of my hosts, I waited for a few unending hours for Aliah to arrive.

Aliah arrived with a Maruti Van by 10.30 a.m. on the same day. She said that she knew somebody in Bandipora where I could stay safely and get treated. We lodged with a man called Haseen Ali in Bandipora. Aliah was visibly shaken seeing my condition and repeatedly insisted upon Haseen Ali to take good care of me. Once she was convinced that Haseen would do his best to look after me and get me treated, she left after pacifying me through her sobs. How much I loved this girl! Had I not been required to go back to my village in Neelum Valley, I would have got married to her straightaway. But I needed to go back to Abbu and Ammi first.

The eye specialist at Bandipora examined my eyes. I had told him that I had injured myself while playing cricket in a village, where I had come to visit my uncle from Kupwara. The ball had hit a window pane and the shattered shards had flown in and hit my eyes. He gave me some medicines, but said a restorative surgery would be required to correct my vision and heal the wound properly. It would only be possible in Srinagar. The medicines reduced the pain and discomfort to some extent, but they would come back as soon as the effect of the medicines subsided. I consulted with Aliah and Haseen Ali and decided to go to Srinagar for the treatment. I was not too keen to roam around, but Haseen assured me that I would be safe in Srinagar with people he knew very well. Aliah seemed to trust Haseen Ali like her elder brother. Also, in that condition, I would not be able to make the journey back home.

My movements were only known to Aliah now. I asked her not to disclose anything to Shahid in case he contacted her. I had switched off my mobile so that nobody from the Jihad Council could track me.

Srinagar

Aliah had not accompanied me to Srinagar. It would raise suspicion and I did not want her to be in any kind of danger. Haseen Ali handed me over to Mansoor Dar, a professor in the

Government College and had left. My eyesight had dwindled, a lot in last few days and everything seemed quite blurry. Two doctors in Srinagar examined me and said the surgery required would not be possible even in Srinagar. Only the Army Hospital had the specialisation in terms of surgeons and equipment to carry out a very intricate surgery to mend the retina of the right eye. Or else I would be required to go to a place like Delhi, the capital of this country.

Neither was possible for me. I was dejected and worried. Was this the end of the road? Would I never be able to see my parents again? The small, beautiful village where I had been born and grown up playing with other children? The beauty of bountiful nature, the snow topped cliffs kissing the blue horizon? The small brook that flowed by the side of my village and then walking along it to reach the banks of the ethereal Neelum river.

I was convinced both by Mansoor Dar and Aliah to go the Army Hospital in Srinagar for the treatment.

"Aap befikr rahein..." Mansoor had patted on my shoulder to add that nobody in the hospital would care to check my antecedents. They treated hundreds of civilian patients like me every day and were only concerned about the treatment.

When I had expressed concern that if the people could know about me from the nature of my injury, Mansoor Sahab said that he would vouch for me being a common man and they would not cast aspersion on an established person like him in the society whom they had known for long.

Mansoor Sahab also suggested I change my name to Bashir, a nephew of his who was studying in some other part of the country.

We waited at the reception area for the eye surgeon to see me in the Army Base Hospital in Srinagar. Mansoor pointed out at large number of common people waiting for their turns at various places in the premises of the hospital. He said the army authorities never refused anyone and did their best to treat each person.

Many seemed to know Mansoor Dar and came to greet him. They exchanged pleasantries and smiled at me. There were stories of healing everywhere. A middle-aged man named Yousuf commented on how timely intervention by the doctors here had saved the life of his father who had severe pneumonia. Another couple carrying a baby on a pram informed us that they could become parents, courtesy the expertise of the gynecologist madam in the hospital.

I watched through my teary eyes the doctors and nurses in army uniforms walking past us. What I could not see clearly registered with me through my ears. Some fervent prayers for good treatment of the ill persons, and some voices expressing gratitude for the healing received. A soldier walked up to us and poured some medicine drops into my eyes.

I could not help but ask Mansoor Sahab the reason behind this gesture of the army. He said that they wanted to win over the people foremost by love and compassion.

"Goliyan toh bahut chali beta...kuch aap logon ne maara... kuch inhone. Par masle ke hal pyar mohabbat se hi hota hain. Yeh awam, yeh fauj wahi kar raha hai.

(Many bullets have been fired so far son, some you people have killed while some they had to, but the bitterness can be solved only through love and peace. And this country, this military is doing that.)"

Our conversation was interrupted by the sound of my adopted name being called out.

"Bashir Sheik..."

We entered the chamber of the doctor. A middle-aged balding man whose face I could not see properly greeted us and asked me to lay down on the bed in one side of the room. He asked me the problem I was facing and how had I injured my eyes. I narrated as discussed earlier with Mansoor Sahab. Did I see a faint smile on the face of the doctor who had by then started peering into my eyes through a telescopic lens? I did not not know if he believed my version, but he did not further harp on the topic.

After the examination was over, he said that surgery would be needed soon. The more it was delayed, the greater would be the chances of losing the vision completely.

I was operated upon the next day and stayed put in the hospital for four days before being discharged. The day I was leaving for Mansoor Sahab's house, the dressing of my eyes was removed. As my eyes adjusted to the ambient light, I saw his face. Calm, smiling and reassuring. Yes, the doctor who had operated upon my eyes and given me new vision. As the kind eyes looked at me questioningly, this so called infidel as he would be branded by the hate-mongering Jihadis, Dr Naresh Sinha – the clean shaven, bald and bespectacled man – had become my Khuda, cutting across all barriers of religions and animosities associated with it.

I returned to Mansoor Dar's house and cried. Yes, I had sinned a lot. I claim that responsibility, but that day, I just wanted to repent. There could not be any greater revenge acted upon you than being given a second life by your purported enemies. It was a true jihad of love and sympathy that these so-called Kafir Hindustani soldiers were carrying out against us.

Fifteen days have passed since then. Yesterday the doctor had re-examined me and declared me fit to resume a normal life with some medicines and a few restrictions. The army had not charged a single penny for the treatment.

I spoke to Aliah and she was beaming with happiness. She wanted to come over and meet me. I have stopped her and said that I would come back on my own. My eyes have opened up. My mother had said to always look for the truth before committing to a cause. I had failed then, but now I see the truth. My vision has truly been restored.

I have decided to start my homeward journey tomorrow. It's better not to meet Aliah now as I may be tracked by the jihadi members. They might have become suspicious of my intentions as I had gone underground. She has been convinced after some persuasion from me. I shall arrange for her joining me in PoK soon after I settle down there. I will call Karim once more and tie up the crossing back.

22

Zahir's Diary

On the way back
6th January

One more day on this side of the LoC. The kind of love and affection I have received from Karim and his parents are no less than what I get from my own family. The environment in the house is a bit sombre as I shall be leaving tomorrow. Ammi has made special dishes for me today. They were all in agreement with my decision of going back. I have not spoken about Aliah to them, but Karim knows.

The last few days, he has stuck to me like a shadow probing me for all the details since he had left me. I shared with him all the details and have given him the diary to read. I told him that I have found the truth.

It is mindless violence that is being perpetrated by Pakistani jihadis from the other side. People in Kashmir valley by and large are happy with the idea of staying with Hindustan. Actually, it had never mattered to them till the Pakistanis started poisoning the minds of the youths in the valley with radicalism. Kashmiris are a peaceful lot. They are not obsessed with fighting, rivalry and killing, like some of the tribes of Pakistan and Afghanistan. They deserve to live peacefully. The Indian Army and the government are taking very good care of these people, unlike on our side. And they have suffered a lot over the last few years. It is time that the jihadis from across the border leave them alone to live peacefully.

I am a small fry, yet I shall go back and try to drive across this point to the honchos of LeT and JeM. It is a lost cause they are fighting, leading to innocent people like Abid and Jehangir losing their lives for no reason.

We were again watching the video clips of the atrocities shared by the Jihad Council. After having seen the Indian Army personnel from close quarters, I am now very sure that the blurred and hazy figures in the clips could be anyone but the Indian Army soldiers. They do not wear the kind of uniforms donned by the soldiers in the clips. These are all fake videos or of events in some other countries and definitely not from Kashmir. And not all the soldiers in India are dark skinned as has been told to us when we had questioned the complexion of the soldiers in the video clips. Another lie fed to ignorant youths like us.

I also suddenly remembered the giggling man who was being thrashed while hanging upside down from a tree in the training camp in Balakote. Well, it makes sense now. In fact, in one of the clips, the area where so called Indian soldiers were shot to be terrorising Kashmiris seemed familiar. These people were shooting fake videos in that hidden enclosure behind the madrasa and using them to instigate innocent people.

We have to get ready early tomorrow morning. I shall let Karim read whatever I have written so far.

23

The truth but the truth

A month had passed off peacefully in Karim's life. Zeenat had visited him once to return the diary. But Karim has not been able to post it back to Zahir yet. In fact, he did not hear from Zahir since he had crossed over. Sometimes he thought of locating Masood, the handler and finding out if he held any information about Zahir. But he refrained from getting back in touch with a guy who had such dubious credentials.

Life had already started showing him brighter prospects. He had officially surrendered to the Army authorities about ten days back. As a measure of support to return to normal life, he had been given an option to join the Indian Army as a soldier in a Light Infantry Regiment. He came to know that many youths like him who had gone astray on the paths of terrorism were given this opportunity to resettle in their lives. He had consulted with his parents and accepted the offer. A government job, prospect of visiting various parts of India, good pay and free medical facilities for oneself and parents, accommodation, schooling for children, subsidised items through CSD the service provided it all. And the biggest advantage was that it would provide *izzat* in the society. He would be looked up to by many youths in his village and the neighbouring ones, and many would get motivated by him.

He was seated in a small office inside the Kupwara military camp. He had been personally called by Col Manav and Capt Zeenat to complete the formalities related to joining in the training. Karim was amazed at the sight of the Army cantonment. Spick and span wide roads, sprawling bungalows and barracks systematically perched on the levelled slopes of the mountains and the disciplined movement of men and vehicles all bore the picture of a methodical, yet harmonious life. It was discipline at its best.

Zeenat entered the office sporting white trousers and a jacket. She was perspiring in spite of the cold temperature outside. Inside the compact office space, it was comfortable owing to the portable blower emitting warm air. She occupied her chair and announced that she had just completed an engrossing game of basketball with the troops. The sweat trickled down her rosy cheeks glistening in the fading lights of the approaching evening. Her hair was tied in a small bun and she looked ethereal in her usual not so feminine avatar.

Zeenat looked at Karim for a few moments before taking out a sheaf of papers from the drawer of her office table. She handed them over to Karim and softly asked him to read. It was a letter written in Urdu. Karim started reading it. Translated to English it would be like this:

Dear Aliah,

You must have felt terribly hurt when you realised that I had left without meeting you. After all you have done for me, it was really wrong on my part to have disappeared like that. But trust me dear, it was your safety that was in my mind foremost. In this dangerous game of deceit and intrigue, it was only you I trusted and could not afford to lose. I had lost all trust in my peers with whom I had stayed and operated during the last one year in Kashmir. I could not trust anyone apart from you and Karim.

And I promise you, my dear, that if I live, I will soon come back to you and bring you back to my place as my wife.

You will be happy to know that I had crossed over courtesy Karim's help, but not before being almost hunted down by the army. I do not know how Karim is because he was also involved in a firefight during the migration. Do try to find out about him. My eyes have healed perfectly.

Had it not been for you and the doctor sahib of the Srinagar Army Hospital, I would not be writing this letter to you, sitting in my house. Doctor Sahab is the angel that Khuda sent my way and you led me to him. I got new eyes and a conscience which had been blinded by the radicals back here in my home place. What mayhem I had been sent to cause in the Kupwara-Sopore area! No matter how much I repent, I can't bring back all the innocent people who have lost their lives. I deserved to die. But god must have kept me alive for a reason. Redemption, I say.

The Kashmiris don't need us. They want to live happily and peacefully. This entire theory of oppression being propagated by the jihadis from this side is baseless. I have seen it in the pained eyes of the old woman who has lost her son and heard the helpless father's anguish at the untimely loss of his only son to this so-called jihad. Generations have wasted themselves flung into a cause which has been non-existent. People have suffered. People have been cheated.

The fact is, Aliah, this entire thing has become a business here. The Jihad Council lives off the money Pakistanis send them to promote the secessionist movement in Kashmir. It generates income for them. It is their livelihood. Till the time the issue of Kashmir lives, these ill-educated ultra-radical mullahs and maulavis will live luxuriously. They do not have any other skill to survive upon, except for blind hatred for others, which they sell to run an industry of killing and massacre at the behest of the Pakistan army. And the Pakistan army justifies its existence by promoting these barbarians, brainwashing innocent youths on either side of the LoC.

They are least bothered about the Kashmiris. Neither do they have any loyalty to Pakistanis. They owe their allegiance to money and wealth that they have been amassing. While their children go abroad to get educated, they are pushing others' kids into this mindless game of death and devastation.

Once the Jihad Council got to know about my return, they asked me to report to them. They had written me off their roster. In fact, they had even told my parents that I had been captured by Indian security forces and did not pay a single penny as promised earlier. They said that till the time there was no confirmation about my whereabouts, they would not shell out any money.

They wanted to felicitate me for the excellent way in which I had carried out militancy in Kashmir. I did not know what their agenda was, but I decided to go and meet them in the Balakote Madrasa.

Top brass of the council were present, decked up in finest of imported attires with itr and surma. Aliah, by looking at them, no one can can say that these sophisticated looking men are actually harbingers of such devastation and carnage for fellow human beings. They hugged me and kissed my forehead, describing me as a farishta, presenting me as an epitome of jihad against the kafir in front of another batch of recruits waiting to be inducted into India. I looked at their innocent faces, some of which have not yet started to yield a beard and spotted the shimmering fanaticism in the eyes that have been drilled in by these hatemongers. I cringed at their slimy touch and felt all the innocent souls who had perished due to my acts were staring down upon me from the skies.

I festered at the repeated mention of the word 'kafir'. These radical zealots had probably never interacted with non-muslims in their life. I stood there by the grace of an Indian and I could not tolerate it any further. I confronted them. I called a spade a spade and urged them to stop sending young innocent people like us to die for a cause that was not there. I told them that it was a grave sin they were committing. But these Jihadis are so manipulative that even the Almighty cannot convince them. They value money above everything. I tried to redeem myself, Aliah, nevertheless. I know that

I could have silently settled somewhere else on this side of Kashmir, but I wanted to face these cowards and slap them hard on their faces.

The whole assembly did not know what had come down upon them. I turned a villain within minutes and was banished within no time. Before leaving, I observed some young petrified eyes following my retreating steps. I wish if I could have shown light to some of our naïve youths sitting there in the madrasa, on the threshold of a bleak troubled future. They have threatened me with dire consequences, but I do not care.

At least I am happy to be back with Abbu and Ammi in the quiet little village I call home. I shall plan something, Aliah and reach out to you soon. We shall be together and create our own home. Our little heaven on this earth far away from the maddening violence and hatred. Till then, do take care of yourself, my love.

Do not share anything with Shahid or any other members from my former team. It is better if you stay away from them completely.

Love you a lot.
Yours forever,
Zahir

Karim folded the letter and looked back at Zeenat inquisitively. The question was obvious.

Then he observed something that sent a chill down his spine. Zeenat had taken off the jacket and had a white collared tee shirt beneath it. A small red mole shone below the Adam's apple, wetted by the stream of sweat dripping down the throat.

"A... Aliah?" was all that his hoarse voice could manage.

The unquivering gaze, travelling from the still eyes as blue and placid as the surface of the Wular Lake on a breezeless summer day, was devoid of any emotion.

"Captain Zeenat Mirza, alias Aliah," she replied.

Karim was not in a state to speak. Zeenat offered him a glass of water and continued.

"I am in the Military Intelligence Corps, Karim. We had infiltrated the team of Zahir. These youngsters from the other side are always driven by enthusiasm, but lack the sharpness to deal with ploys, the reason they fall prey to the Pakistani jihadis. From the day Zahir came across me in the town of Sopore, his every move was being tracked. I lived there as Aliah Pundit, who actually belonged to Baramullah area and then had migrated to study outside. My intelligence team and I had the authority that allowed me to impersonate her after taking few people in the village in confidence. So, when Zahir had tried to get my credentials verified, we led his contacts to the men who would speak on our behalf. The coaching centre in Sopore where I had enrolled is funded by Army so that didn't pose to be a problem.

"I befriended Zahir and overcame the suspicion of Shahid. Zahir did not know, but Shahid was also trying to get friendly with me. A little confidence instilled from my side revealed quite interesting agendas. I came to know how Shahid was playing another game to dethrone Zahir and become the area commander. My team and I capitalised on that latent feud and tried to disperse the group."

"Your team?" asked a dumbfounded Karim.

"Yes, you have heard about the stone pelters from Zahir, right? We had two boys from our intelligence team who formed a part of the stone pelting group. They had been selected by Zahir and Shahid to be indoctrinated and become militants. They were part of meetings and gatherings and kept me informed."

Zeenat continued.

"Well, Shahid was on his own mission. He was getting impatient as probably he had sensed the turmoil inside Zahir about the purpose of the jihad. He went berserk. He tried to get Abid, the engineer, killed by providing incorrect information about the number of persons present in the CRPF camp on the night of the attack. When it failed, he eliminated Abid himself. He tipped off the army about Zahir's hiding place and he was cordoned off. But after that I took good care of him and ensured he lived and got treated."

"But why did you or your team not kill Zahir?" Karim finally managed to ask.

"Zahir's days were numbered since the day he joined the ranks of the terrorists. He would get killed either this side, or on the other side of the LoC. But here, our aim is not to kill unnecessarily, Karim. We try to reform. And in Zahir's case, we wanted to see how and from where he had come in. We wanted to trace his roots. See, killing him would have been very easy. He had no one on this side of the border. But firstly, he was a reformed man who had seen the truth about Kashmir and we wanted him to go back as a messenger to the jihadis on the other side. Secondly, we wanted to check out the routes and the people who assisted these infiltrations from our side. That's how we reached you, isn't it, Karim? Aren't you too a reformed youth now? Can't say whether Zahir would get a job with the Pakistani security forces, but you are being provided respectable employment."

There was a warm smile on her face. Karim nodded his head in affirmation.

"But on the day Zahir was crossing back to PoK, when we got caught in a firefight with the army, was that planned?"

"Of course, my friend. It was me who had tipped off the local unit about the crossing. Zahir had never been left unmonitored since the time he had bumped into me. You must have read about the stone pelters in the diary. We had our members amongst them and two of them had been selected personally by Shahid to be led into militancy. So we kept getting a lot of inputs about Zahir and Shahid. While Zahir crossed over to PoK, Shahid was tracked and hunted down with another guy called Bilawal from Sonmarg. Again, an excellent clandestine operation by our team.

She then placed the letter inside the drawer of the table and continued in an unflinching tone.

"Five days back, a twenty-three year old youth called Zahir hailing from the Dossud village in Neelum Valley has been reported missing. The local police is carrying out investigations, but there has been no progress so far – Radio Pakistan, Muzaffarabad reports." Zeenat curved her shoulders in a gesture of helplessness and slided a printout with the news scribbled on it in Urdu.

Karim felt as if the ground under his feet had been moved away. It was the same sinking feeling he had had when he had fallen into the deep ravine. As Capt Zeenat stood up from her chair, Karim understood it was time to leave. He proceeded for the door and stared at those beautiful, yet dangerous blue eyes once more. He could read the words behind the unwavering stare.

"You got a second life, Karim. Live it. Zahir did not."

24

IRIS and aftermath

A day later, Zeenat was summoned by Col Manav to his office. When she entered the cabin, Manav greeted her with a warm smile and pointed to the chair opposite his across the big mahogany table.

As Zeenat occupied the chair, she noticed a bearded youth sitting on the sofa kept in the corner of the room. He looked like a typical Kashmiri fellow in the local attire. Tall, fair and sporting a beard and a long mane, he came across as a saint to her.

"So Zeenat err...Iris, get your bags packed." Manav quipped at her.

Zeenat stared with inquisitive eyes as a phrase like this in armed forces dictionary hinted at a posting to another place.

Manav sensed the jolt in Zeenat and assured her.

"Ha ha...there, I caught you! Don't worry. The bosses are quite happy with the first outcome of operation Zeenat. You will be accompanying me to the Corps HQ and further to New Delhi for a briefing on the ops."

Zeenat heaved a sigh of relief and smiled. "When do we move, sir?"

"In a couple of days dear. Till then, I want you to brief Maj Jay Shergill about the in and outs of the operation planned by you. Hand him over important contacts and other necessary stuff..." As Manav gestured the young man seated on the sofa, he walked across to Zeenat.

Zeenat greeted him and in spite of being a much trained int operative could not help but appreciate the demeanor of the Officer. He had merged into his character with such perfection that even Zeenat had failed to identify a possible disguise.

"When do we start, sir?" Zeenat asked Maj Shergill.

Shergill flashed a bright charming smile through the dense brown growths on his face and replied. "Right away, Captain. From Iris to Adonis, we move on... with your permission Manav sir."

Manav laughed heartily and stood up from his chair, dismissing the youngsters.

"Permission granted..."

This operation continued. Combat has many dimensions. Psychology is one of the most important aspects among these. Various methods are devised to erase the sense of alienation for India that had been imposed in the mind of the Kashmiris by the Pakistani agencies. Also, it augurs well to give back to the Jihadis a taste of their own medicine by sending across a message of reform that was happening in the valley. Changing the psyche of the mass this side of the border automatically had an effect on the perpetrators across.

This was considered as a psychological blow when many Mujahids like Zahir despatched by the Jihadi Council either deserted the ranks soon after recruitment or went back to confront the JeM and the LeT leaders for jeopardizing their lives for a non-committal cause.

Iris is the Goddess of messages as per the Greek mythology. Capt Zeenat, instrumental in infiltrating the mujahideeen network was coded as Iris, who delivered hard-hitting counter measures to the Jihadi Council across the LoC.

Zahir was suspected to have been eliminated by the Jihadi Council in Pakistan. Karim Wani joined the Indian Army after a year-long training in a Light Infantry Regimental Centre. While some of the events in this book are inspired by true events, the conceptualization of the storyline has been fictionalized for making it interesting for readers. All the names of the characters have been changed to protect identities.

It takes love, compassion and empathy to eradicate radicalism from the minds of the vitiated society. The Indian Army has been dealing with the situation on ground, armed not only by arms and ammunition, but the softer skills which remain largely invisible. We hope that one day very soon, this truth will prevail over everything else and Kashmir will shine as the jewel in the crown of India, like earlier times.

List of acronyms

2IC – Second in Command
BSF – Border Security Force
CBMs – Confidence Building Measures
CRPF – Central Reserve Police Force
GOC – General Officer Commanding
HEAT – High Explosive Anti-Tank
IMA – Indian Military Academy
JeM – Jaish-e-Mohammad
LAC – Line of Actual Control
LeT – Lashkar-e-Taiba
MPVs – Mine Protected Vehicles
PLA – People's Liberation Army
RPG – Rocket Propelled Grenade
TAR – Tibet Autonomous Region

www.ingramcontent.com/pod-product-compliance
Ingram Content Group UK Ltd.
Pitfield, Milton Keynes, MK11 3LW, UK
UKHW040004200726
13854UKWH00001B/26

9 789395 192323